Contractually Yours

Connie Cox

Copyright 2013

Contractually Yours

Chapter One

"The wedding is off," Brandon D'Estrehan announced as dispassionately as if he were ordering a cup of coffee. "My apologies for the inconvenience."

For the hundredth time in two days, Caroline Duplessis pushed Replay on the DVD player to study the video of the world's most respected and feared international corporate raider calling off his wedding from the altar rail.

The wedding photographer in the vestibule had picked up his deep baritone clearly in the huge St. Louis Cathedral in the heart of New Orleans' French Quarter. D'Estrehan had looked over the diamond-bedecked crowd as stoic as if his face were chiseled from the same stone his heart must have been carved from.

Caroline zoomed in to study his eyes. No blink. No flicker. Nothing but black irises in dark brown pupils staring out over the distinguished well-wishers.

Ruthless. They had called him cold-blooded and ruthless as they filed out of the church.

Caroline just called him *dream killer*.

From the tabloids, she knew the groom had gone back to

business as usual that very evening. The heartbroken bride could not be found.

Caroline glanced down at the sheaf of bills and her extremely small bank balance spread across the coffee table that doubled as a makeshift desk in her home office. Her studio apartment wasn't big enough for a proper desk, even if she could have afforded one. No other way around it, the end of this wedding meant the end of her fledgling wedding planning service, Weddings Divine.

Her phone rang and Caroline jumped, startled at the jangling intrusion on her pity party. Was it another bill collector?

Her best friend since grade school, Paula, was on the line. "Want to do some lunch? The gang's getting together for a nice long girl chat."

The thought of food made Caroline's stomach flop. "No. Not today. Thanks."

"Are you still brooding over the wedding? Honey, there will be other opportunities." While Paula was sympathetic, she didn't understand. Born with a trust fund, Paula worked as a kindergarten teacher because she loved her job, not because she needed her paycheck.

The Winters-D'Estrehan wedding was supposed to be Caroline's big break into the very exclusive and very profitable New Orleans high-society wedding circuit.

Fresh out of business school, Caroline had borrowed every penny she could scrape together, including money from her parents, to get Weddings Divine off the ground, but after two years, she still hadn't been able to penetrate New Orleans' close-knit echelon of founding families.

Also an outsider, Laurel Winters had been willing to give Weddings Divine the break Caroline so desperately needed.

Laurel needed a quick wedding in two months, max. Caroline didn't ask why the need for haste. She didn't need to know. All she knew was that Brandon D'Estrehan's wealth and power made him an international icon.

His success story had graced every financial periodical, every social magazine and every gossip rag to hit the newsstand in the last six months. Phoenix Rising was the most aggressive and the most victorious corporate takeover company in the world. Caroline had planned to piggyback on that fame and fortune to get Weddings Divine into the black.

Paula lowered her tone to a gossip whisper. "Has anyone figured out why he called off the wedding? I haven't seen a word about it in any of the papers."

"I haven't either," Caroline answered vaguely, distracted by unfreezing the video. The camera rolled while guests from all over the world filed out of the cathedral into Jackson Square, tittering under their collective breaths. New Orleans would buzz about this one for months to come.

"I'll bet it was something that bride of his did. She was the worst Bridezilla I've ever seen."

"She was under a lot of pressure. After all, she was a society nobody marrying New Orleans' most eligible bachelor." Caroline had dodged around the paparazzi that tracked every move the fiancée of Brandon D'Estrehan made, doing her best to be invisible while Laurel sparkled like a Baccarat champagne flute.

While Laurel might be the most difficult bride Caroline had ever had to humor, she was also the wealthiest. Or she would have been as soon as she and Brandon D'Estrehan promised to love and cherish unto death did they part.

"How can you defend her?" Paula persisted. "You worked days, nights and weekends. Whenever she crooked her little finger, you were there."

"With all the planning we had to do for a wedding this size, I had to be available every minute Laurel could spare to get the job done." And Caroline had done it well. She had accomplished the impossible, pulling together the wedding of the season in six weeks.

She had been rewarded by at least a half dozen leads for new clients that should have catapulted Weddings Divine over the line from living on borrowed money to making a profit.

"I admit Laurel was difficult to please, but I felt sorry for her. She had no friends or family to help. I don't know what I would do without my mom to help with my wedding when the time comes."

Caroline stared at Brandon D'Estrehan's image on her screen. He continued to stand at the front of the cathedral, immobile, while everyone left. "And the groom wouldn't involve himself in a single decision."

At the time, Caroline had realized how fortunate she was. Her own wedding, should that day ever come, would be so different. Her wedding day would be rich with hugs and kisses from those who wished her the best. And, most of all, she would be marrying a man whose eyes sparkled when she entered the room. Not a man with no joy in his expression. She was determined to wait for Mr. Right no matter how long it took.

"Come to lunch with us. You've worked hard. You need to play," Paula insisted.

"I'm not really in the mood to play." Caroline was too embarrassed to explain her financial mess, especially since the decisions she had made went against all the rules of good business.

"If you change your mind, we'll be at The Court of Two Sisters drinking mimosas and munching on boiled shrimp." Paula rang off, clearly not happy with her friend.

Caroline ran the video back and asked herself once again if she could have done anything to avert this calamity.

On the screen, Brandon D'Estrehan filled the doorway, looking like every bride's dream in his black tuxedo, contrasting white shirt, dark chocolate hair, and olive skin. "Laurel, I must speak to you in private," he said.

That was it. That was the moment all Caroline's excruciatingly detailed plans fell apart.

Laurel had turned into sugar and spice, giving Brandon her best little-girl smile. "We'll have a lifetime to talk after the ceremony. We shouldn't keep our guests waiting any longer."

"I assure you, Laurel, you don't want to have this conversation in front of witnesses." He took his bride's elbow and escorted her out of the room, closing the door behind him.

That was the end for the Winters-D'Estrehan wedding.

And the end of Weddings Divine.

All the prospective clients had cancelled. No bride wanted her big day to be tarnished by association with the biggest wedding scandal of recent memory. And New Orleans society had a very long memory.

Caroline clicked off the video and took a deep sip of her herbal tea to calm her queasy stomach. Her hands shook as she lifted her cup.

She had planned to recover, to rise from the ashes and begin again. She had already resigned herself to starting over on a much smaller scale and begin again the very, very steep climb up the New Orleans social ladder. Until her early morning phone call.

The call from her banker had turned this wedding from socially disastrous into financially catastrophic. Apparently, the extremely large check Laurel had used to pay her final balance the night before the wedding had bounced.

And the payoff for the short-term loan her parents had secured for her using their home as collateral was due within the week.

Caroline popped the DVD out of the player and tucked it into her briefcase. There was no help for it. She would have to look into Brandon D'Estrehan's hard, flat eyes and demand payment from the man who had ruined her dreams.

Brandon hung up the phone with more force than necessary. "We lost the deal."

His lawyer and best friend, Jack, cradled his head in his hands. "Should I ask why?"

"Same as the last one. These little mom-and-pop enterprises don't want to sell out to a playboy." He scrubbed his hand through his hair. "They'd rather close their operation and lay off their employees than hand over their life's work to a womanizer. How in hell did I get that reputation to start with?"

Jack gave his friend a sympathetic smirk. "It's unfair."

"But then, nobody ever promised that life was fair, did they?" Brandon suppressed his anger. It served no purpose.

"Your name and face sells gossip rags. The paparazzi don't worry about truth as much as money." Jack thumped the airtight contract on Brandon's desk. The contract the shop owners refused to sign for sentimental reasons. "You're the most staid, practical-minded man of your age and wealth I've ever known."

It was true. While women always made themselves available when he needed an arm ornament and Brandon enjoyed beautiful female companionship as much as the next red-blooded guy, his heart and soul was Phoenix Rising. He would never let a woman get between him and business.

He picked up a tabloid that had been delivered with the morning mail, scanned the headlines about how his broken marriage put him back on the market, and crumpled it in disgust.

Jack crossed over to the third-story window and looked down at the crowded sidewalk below. "I walked through that mob of women holding Marry Me signs getting to the office this morning. They're worse now than they were before the engagement announcement."

Brandon joined him, glancing past the mob to the hypnotic flow of the muddy Mississippi River less than a block away from his French Quarter office. "Hard to believe that six months ago, only the business world knew about Phoenix Rising."

"That's the price you pay when you're single, photogenic, and shortlisted for *Time* magazine's Man of the Year, not to mention *People Magazine*'s and *Cosmo*'s Most Eligible Bachelors lists."

Taking over companies was like paying poker. The cards a player held counted, but only as much as the attitude the player projected. Brandon had always projected a severe, no-nonsense image to keep up his bluff over the competition. Celebrity fame was not part of that image.

"Threaten them with a lawsuit and get me off their lists."

"Freedom of speech laws being what they are, you're out of luck. There's nothing libelous about printing public facts and photographs along with opinion pieces about what a great matrimonial prospect you are." Jack pointed to the magazines on the credenza. "Have you read the advance copies yet? They're really rather flattering."

"Throw money at the publishers and buy them off, then."

"You can't buy your way around everything, Brandon. Some things aren't for sale." Jack held up a video. "By the way, that last tape of Laurel sobbing outside the cathedral cost you well into six figures to keep out of the public eye. I think we got them all now."

Brandon closed the hurricane shutters, casting the room into shadows, and glared. "Do something, Jack. I've got too many sensitive mergers in the works that require discreetness."

Jack shrugged. "Your engagement was doing the trick. Being a celebrity bachelor doesn't generate nearly as much interest if the bachelor isn't eligible anymore." He shoved the worn, handwritten list at Brandon. "Take a look and pick another one."

"There's got to be a better way."

"If there is, I can't think of it." Jack put the list on Brandon's desk. "Getting married isn't a bad plan. It worked quite well for a while. My apologies again that my staff didn't uncover the scoop on Laurel until it was almost too late. And I blamed your suspicions on your reluctance to get married. Be it blackjack, business or women, your poker sense always seems to be right on. I'll never again doubt your intuition."

Brandon picked up the list and put it down again. "It was an easy mistake to make. Laurel had all the qualities we'd been looking for. She could dazzle with her smile, make small talk with anyone from dockworker to foreign diplomat, and put together an impromptu dinner party for twenty with less than an hour's notice."

Jack smiled. "It didn't hurt that she could make love to a camera better than any Hollywood starlet."

"Yes, she would have been the perfect wife if she hadn't already been married to that octogenarian in Italy."

Jack flipped on the lamp next to the bookcase. "It was still a good plan, wasn't it?"

"I have to admit it was. I completed more deals in the last two weeks with Laurel around to keep the press at bay than I've accomplished in the last three months."

"Then pick another bride." Jack looked his friend in the eyes and promised, "This time I'll listen better when your gambling instincts kick in."

"Me, too." Brandon had made his company a success by studying hard, working harder, and finding the right combination of business acumen and instinct to make the right decisions. He had let his head overrule his gut feeling with Laurel. It was a mistake that wouldn't happen again.

As Jack headed back to his office, Brandon sipped cold coffee and glared at the closed shutters that blocked his view as well as kept out prying telescopic lenses.

He ignored the flashing light on his phone that meant his executive secretary, Mrs. Willoughby, needed his attention as he glanced at the list of prospective brides. Even though he didn't relish the hassle of bride hunting again, his instincts were screaming that marriage was the right way to keep all the paparazzi diverted and get back to business.

Knife-like tension stabbed him between his shoulder blades. He had just enough time for a quick workout in the company gym. Forty-five minutes on the punching bag would clear his head and give him time to shower before his video conference with the CEO of the doomed beverage distribution company.

Phoenix Rising was built on turning bad businesses into good ones, providing jobs when those companies would have closed their doors and keeping food on the table for all the families who would have gone hungry without their paychecks, like his had when his dad lost his job. He would do anything, including sacrifice his unwedded state, to keep Phoenix Rising growing in the right direction. Woe unto anyone who stood in his way.

He opened the door, and there stood Mrs. Willoughby, blocking his exit. Or rather, blocking a petite brunette's entrance.

La petite looked familiar, but Brandon couldn't remember where they might have met. He did a quick mental scan of all the women on his list. They were all blonde, curvaceous, and easy to pick out in a crowd.

Brandon studied the woman he could barely see behind Mrs. Willoughby's solid form.

The woman took a step to the side, and he caught a better glance before Mrs. Willoughby shifted to blockade her again.

She must be scrappier than she appeared. She had breached the barriers of his first-floor security team and now attempted to thwart his mastiff of an executive secretary. And she showed no sign of cowering or trembling.

At his discreet nod, his long-time assistant reluctantly stepped to the side, although Mrs. Willoughby looked ready to throw herself into the breach should she think it necessary.

The best word to describe the intruder's beauty was subtle. She had an understated elegance that a photographer would miss amidst the glitz and glamour that the media preferred.

He inspected her from the top of her sleek mink-brown chin-length hair, onward past her amber eyes so stunning the color had to come from colored contacts, down past her modest breasts, her athletically trim waist and hips to her simple flats. She was the exact opposite of all the women on his list.

She didn't fidget under his inspection. Instead, she simply gave him back the same scrutiny in kind.

She had a quiet, confident presence. *Still waters run deep*, his grandfather would say about this woman.

She reached around Mrs. Willoughby and extended her hand. "Mr. D'Estrehan, I need to speak with you."

He joined his palm to hers, surprised to feel her grip was not as delicate as it looked. He had thought he had become jaded, but now, a spark of interest travelled through him. No. More like a bolt of lightning.

As if she felt it, too, she dropped her hand and rubbed it on her thigh.

"What can I do for you?"

Mrs. Willoughby scowled as she spoke first. "Miss

Duplessis was Laurel Winter's personal wedding planner. She has a DVD she thinks you'll want."

Chapter Two

Caroline had expected his touch to be cold, like his heart. As his fingers brushed hers, a jolt raced up her arm. Her heart rate increased although she fought hard to keep her breathing steady. Was this the charisma all the women fell for? Was she like the screaming masses on the sidewalk she had waded through to get to him?

She rubbed her palm on her thigh to make the tingling stop. Ever so slowly the sensation faded, leaving tickly traces behind.

Had he felt it? That energy between them? Of course not. His face never changed.

No, she would not be attracted to this man. There were plenty of eligible bachelors to be had should she want to find a man. She would not be attracted to the most infamous of them all, a man who could leave his bride at the altar and never look back.

"Please, have a seat, Miss Duplessis." He indicated a Louis XVI chair opposite his desk. If Caroline hadn't worked at an antique shop during college, she might not have realized the chair was authentic. It sat lower to the ground than most modern chairs, leaving him towering over her.

"Coffee? Espresso?" He picked up his oversized mug, cradling it in both hands. No demitasse cup and saucer for him. His large hands would overwhelm delicate china.

"No. Thank you." She certainly didn't want to risk another touch as he handed a drink to her. All she wanted from him was her money.

He propped himself between her chair and his desk, one ankle over the other and arms crossed over his chest, encroaching on her personal space.

"Then let's get on with it."

She would not be intimidated. His coldheartedness didn't run to brides only. He might be the darling of the celebrity magazines, but according to the trade periodicals she subscribed to, he had been responsible for more company owners losing their businesses than any one single man of this decade. If she couldn't convince him to cover Laurel's bounced check, she would soon join their ranks.

Grace and dignity, Caroline, she bolstered herself. Grace and dignity.

Instead of looking up into those flat, brown eyes, she pulled a photocopy of a cancelled check from her briefcase. No sense in sugarcoating with this man. "The check I received to pay for your wedding has been reversed for insufficient funds."

"My *cancelled* wedding, Miss Duplessis?"

"Yes, your *cancelled* wedding."

"Do you have a copy of the contract?"

She shuffled through catering plans and florist estimates until she found the document. "I think you'll find it in order."

Making sure to keep the distance of the paper between their hands, she fumbled as she handed it over. His eyes met hers, mesmerizing her like a snake before it struck. She couldn't look away.

He broke the spell when he reached behind him and snagged a pair of reading glasses from his desktop.

"According to the contract, Weddings Diving must receive payment in full before any services are rendered."

"Yes. That's correct." Caroline kept her chin up, even though he had just put his finger on the pulse of her mistake.

"How long have you been in business, Miss Duplessis?"

Caroline thought about all that his deceptively simple question intimated. She didn't want to justify her business decisions to him, but he held the purse strings. At least he hadn't sent her packing empty-handed yet.

"Weddings Divine is less than two years old, but that doesn't mean I don't provide excellent service. I have years of experience behind me. My mother owned a bridal gown shop for years and offered bridal advice as well. I worked with her all throughout my teens. From her shop, we planned hundreds of weddings. Then during college I worked for an antique dealer who set up weddings at antebellum houses as a side business. I know a lot about wedding planning." She finally stopped herself. She had intended to explain, not rattle off her life's story.

"But not a lot about business. What happened, Miss Duplessis?" Had his tone softened? Was that a touch of kindness in his voice?

"Laurel asked me to hold the check until the day of the wedding. She said that a joint account would be opened for her and the money would be transferred to cover the expenses."

"You must be a longtime friend of Laurel's to extend such a generous offer." No warmth in that question. She must have imagined his earlier tone.

Was he accusing her of something?

The billion-dollar question loomed large. Why had he called off the wedding?

Caroline took a deep breath and confessed her poor

business decision. "I wasn't acquainted with her at all until she contacted me about planning her wedding. I took a chance because I thought this would be my big break into society weddings."

"Not meaning to insult Weddings Divine, but why do you think Laurel chose such a small, unproven establishment to plan such a large affair?"

"She said the wedding needed to happen as quickly as possible. Of course, I didn't ask why, but she implied...well, I assumed..." Caroline broke off, not sure how to go on.

He had no such hesitation. "There was no child." His eyes reflected like shards of broken glass. This first sign of emotion was so intense the air crackled between them.

She believed him. She didn't know why. Maybe it was his direct stare or the way he met her head-on. Or maybe it was that elusive charisma again. Everything about him, even his bluntness, indicated that he was the type of man who would never stoop to lying.

Whatever the reason, Caroline mentally erased one of the sins she had tallied against him.

Under his intense stare, she felt compelled to explain further.

"The more established wedding planners would have been booked months in advance. I only had a few weddings scheduled, and they were rather simple, so I told Laurel I could put together the kind of wedding she wanted in such a short time." Caroline pushed back her shoulders. "And I did. It would have been a wonderful wedding if you hadn't called it off."

He lifted an eyebrow at her censoring tone but ignored her unanswered question. "These long hours are what has resulted in such a large invoice, I presume?"

Caroline was forced to admit her business acumen was even worse than she first confessed. "Those charges are not just for my time. Usually, the bride pays the vendors as she signs contracts, but for Lauren, I fronted the money for the caterer, the florist, the photographer, the rehearsal banquet…everything."

"Why would you do that, Miss Duplessis?"

"Laurel didn't seem to have anyone, any family to help with the decisions or the bills. She said she wouldn't have the money until after the wedding, but then assured me you would take care of it. I know that's not how it's usually done, but I wanted to help her. She was so persuasive." Caroline let a tight, ironic smile escape. "And the publicity would have launched Weddings Divine into the upper echelon in profits as well as prestige."

"Yes, I understand. A calculated business risk. I've made a few of them myself. And I've firsthand knowledge of Laurel's persuasiveness."

A great weight lifted from her chest as he gave her hope. "Yes, that's it exactly."

"Did you notice Laurel's signature on the contract, Miss Duplessis?" He held the paper and pointed to the loopy handwriting.

"Yes, of course."

"You do realize that's her name, not mine, and I'm not liable for any expenses incurred in this contract, don't you?"

Caroline felt as if his fist had reached past her chest and closed around her heart. She swallowed past the clenching pain. "But you're the one who called off the wedding. Don't you feel any responsibility?"

She made the mistake of letting her pleading eyes meet his impassive ones. No, he didn't feel responsibility. The man didn't feel anything at all.

"Have you ever played poker, Miss Duplessis?"

"Not much." Where was this going?

"I've played since I was old enough to hold the cards. It's

a family tradition. In fact, it's how my grandfather made his fortune and how my father lost his."

"What does that have to do with my invoice, Mr. D'Estrehan?"

"The most difficult strategy to learn is to know when to fold and walk away from the game."

"Are you suggesting that I write off this loss, Mr. D'Estrehan?"

"Yes, I am."

"Perhaps you don't understand, or more likely, you don't care, but I'll explain it to you anyway." She stood, leaving less than three inches between her chest and his.

The energy surrounding them raised the hair on her arms. "I'm still paying back the loan I took out to open Weddings Divine. My parents put up their home as collateral. I don't have the assets to secure another loan." Caroline wiped at the tears that had begun to roll down her face and wished she could stop them. But they continued to trickle despite her best resolve. "But then, my financial distress isn't your concern, is it?"

She snagged her briefcase from the chair and turned to leave.

"Wait." He reached out to her, his fingers inches from her arm.

She stared at those fingers until he let his arm fall. "Why?"

"What about the DVD? Aren't you going to make me a deal?"

She reached into the outside pocket of her briefcase, pulled out the DVD and put it in the chair to avoid contact with his charismatic touch. "I may not be the businessperson you are, Mr. D'Estrehan, but I'm no blackmailer."

With that, she headed for the door, but his hand on her shoulder stopped her.

Standing so close she could feel his breath on her neck, he said, "In that case, I have a proposition for you, Miss Duplessis. A proposition we can both benefit from."

She turned to face him. "I believe I've just been played, Mr. D'Estrehan. Is this what you call a bluff?"

He flashed her a smile.

Caroline was astonished. She didn't think his lips could curve upward. Not only was she shocked to see his smile, but also his dimple and a glint in his eyes. It was gone before she could react, leaving her thinking she had just imagined it.

"You know more about poker than you let on, Miss Duplessis."

She wanted so badly to walk away and close the door behind her. But the debts in her briefcase weighed heavily on her mind, especially with her parents' house at risk.

"I'm calling your hand, Mr. D'Estrehan. Show me what you have."

"Please, sit." He gestured toward the chair she had just vacated. Caroline expected him to stand over her while she sat and listened, but he surprised her by pulling up a matching chair next to hers. "I'm offering you a partnership in a venture that is very important to me."

"Why?" She didn't bother to hide the reservation in her voice. "You've already thoroughly pointed out my lack of entrepreneurial expertise." Every sensible cell in her body urged her to leave. Any man who could bring her across the gamut of emotions that Brandon D'Estrehan had manipulated her through in the last twenty minutes was not to be trusted.

But she couldn't suppress the spark of hope that sprang from deep within her. To have a second chance to make Weddings Divine solvent, to pay off her loans and have her parents' home secure once again was too good of a chance to pass up without even giving his plan a listen.

She looked him straight in the eyes. Yes, she could ignore

his devastating handsomeness. She could resist that charisma he exuded. She could keep herself from being dominated by his power. She could be his partner and keep Weddings Divine alive.

"What are you proposing, Mr. D'Estrehan?"

He leaned in close to her. "Marriage."

"Pardon? I'm not sure I heard you right?"

"Marriage, Miss Duplessis." He cocked a sardonic eyebrow at her. "Wedded bliss."

Chapter Three

That's what Caroline thought she had heard. Her blood pressure shot up as she realized he had dashed her hopes once again. Her knees brushed his as she stood to go. She had to forget the heat that warmed her solar plexus. Forget Weddings Divine. Forget Brandon D'Estrehan and remember how to breathe.

Brandon stood with her, but she refused to step back even as he towered over her. Instead, she found herself shoving her briefcase between them as she looked up and all but whispered, "What kind of man are you? You just walked out on a wedding. Do you get your kicks from loving and leaving?"

A muscle jumped in his jaw. She expected him to escort her out of his office immediately. Instead, he took a deep breath and walked away from her, putting his desk between them, although he didn't sit. Instead, he picked up a tattered paper on his desk then set it down again.

"The marriage would purely be a business merger, just as the one with Laurel would have been." His tone bordered on a growl as he met her stare. "You have no reason to trust me, but let me assure you that walking away from the deal Laurel and I had struck was not an option I could avoid."

She didn't have reason to trust him, but against her better judgment, she did.

He held up his hand, stalling the myriad of questions that filled her. "I will promise to make our partnership worth your while. We can even put a time limit on it, if you like."

He scribbled on a memo pad and held the slip of paper out to her. She leaned over his desk to take it from him, being careful to touch only the paper.

The dollar figure was more than she could hope to earn with Weddings Divine in the next three years. She laid it across his desk. "I believe you've added too many zeroes here."

He glanced at the note. "No. That's my offer. Be my wife for six months and the money is yours. In the meantime, I'll pay off all your debts."

Caroline stared at the paper as if the numbers would change as she studied it. His offer would solve so many problems. After six months, not only would her bank account be healthy enough to revive her business but she would have also gained the social status to penetrate the highest stratum of New Orleans society.

She ignored the warnings her intuition was sending through her central nervous system and went with the logic her mind was calculating. "Why do you need a wife, Mr. D'Estrehan?"

He walked to his credenza to gather a few magazines. "These are why I need a wife." He thrust them at her as if they repelled him.

She jerked her hand away before he could make contact, letting the handful fall to the floor. Before he could pick them up for her, she bent over and scooped them together. Trying to regain her composure, she studied the cover of one of the magazines.

His pose was striking. Arms crossed over his chest, eyes staring intently into the camera with no hint of who the man was behind the stoic expression.

He looked down at her now with that same unrevealing expression. "The notoriety is keeping me from doing business. You saw the mob on the sidewalk when you entered my building. All this media frenzy makes my private life null and void as well. If I had a wife, this nonsense would go away."

She flipped through a tabloid that showed a grainy photo of Brandon running along the river in very short runner's shorts. She held it up to him.

"This one is very flattering. With recommendations like these, I shouldn't think you would have any trouble finding a wife without having to offer her any recompense."

"Thank you." The slightest quirk of his mouth lasted long enough that she could assure herself it had happened. He swept a hand at the magazines she held. "The prospects these articles generate aren't the types of female who would make a good wife for me."

"What makes you think I'm the type of female who would make a good wife for you?" Caroline narrowed her eyes at him. "And will you decide, the day of the wedding, that I'm not the type you wanted after all?"

"Touché, Miss Duplessis." He sipped his coffee. "Despite those glowing articles, I do make occasional business mistakes. But I learn and recover from them. I'm giving you a chance to recover, too."

"So my job is to keep you safe from other women?"

A full-fledged smile flitted across his eyes and settled into the corners of his lips. He looked approachable, sociable, and very, very handsome. The transformation was so startling that all Caroline could do was stare.

"Yes."

If he showed his private side more, she could probably

make this work. And the money. Heaven knew she needed the money. Six months. That's all it would take. Six months of waking up next to him every morning.

Oh, wait. Would her bargain include *that*? There were some things money could *not* buy. But dimples like his could purchase a lot more than coin. And deep down inside her, a little voice asked, *In the end, what if six months isn't enough?* She realized she was staring when he interrupted her musings.

"Are you sure you don't want a cup of coffee?"

"Yes, I think I would." She dropped into the chair.

He turned toward the coffee bar and grabbed a mug. When he pointed to the Grand Marnier, she nodded.

He poured in a liberal splash of the liqueur and handed her the cup. This time, she deliberately touched him. Yes, no doubt about it. Thrilling buzz each and every time.

"What would you expect from me?" She sipped, then wished she hadn't when the coffee burnt her tongue.

He ticked off her duties on his fingertips. "You will host dinner parties for associates and their spouses, sometimes with very little notice. You will accompany me to various social functions I have to attend. You will be my proxy and attend to the charities I sponsor, go to banquets, hand out awards, that sort of thing. You will be seen in public with me enough to convince the world our marriage is sound, especially around women who would try to come between us."

"Really, Mr. D'Estrehan. You don't think any woman would be so brash as to—" She broke off as she remembered the crowd on the street below.

She looked down into her coffee, took a cautious sip, and after she could stall no longer, asked, "What would you expect from me in private?"

He took a sip of his own coffee as if swallowing down the first answer that came to mind. "I would ask that you refrain from involvement of a personal nature during the time we are together. I'm sure you would be discreet, but the paparazzi would ferret out any hint of an unhappy marriage and would take great joy in blasting it across the media."

She tried to find a better way to word her next question then just bluntly blurted it out, "What about *your* private life?"

He laughed, deep and sincere. "I like you, Miss Duplessis. I think we would do very well together."

Still, he didn't answer the question, and Caroline couldn't find the chutzpah to ask again.

He took an obvious glance at his watch and stood. She stood, too.

That was a lot of money. It would solve a lot of problems, chief among them her parents' loan foreclosure.

"Yes. I'll marry you."

"It's a deal then." He offered his hand and she placed her palm in his. She was fairly certain the tingle she felt wasn't coming just from her bank account.

He gave no sign he felt the same.

Brandon escorted her to the door, clearly ready to see her out now that the deal was struck.

Before he opened the door, he stopped her. "I'll have the prenuptial agreement ready for you to read through by this evening. We'll meet at my home around seven thirty, and you can have a look around while you're there. Will this arrangement work for you?"

Stunned at how quickly his plans were moving forward, Caroline agreed with a vacant nod. "Yes. I'll be there."

"Excellent. Mrs. Willoughby will give you directions." He took another look at his watch, opened the door, and escorted her to the anteroom. "Now, if you'll excuse me, I have a teleconference scheduled."

With that, he left her facing his formidable secretary.

Disappointment rushed over her in a wave. What had she expected? A kiss to seal the deal?

But then, this was strictly business, and business partners didn't kiss—or anything else, either, right?

Chapter Four

Brandon disconnected the video conference on his end and watched his monitor go blank. With another lucrative acquisition behind him, he sat back in his chair and took a rare moment to reflect.

Phone calls needed answering. Stock markets needed studying, and business reports needed analyzing. But right now, he simply sat.

He'd had to exert a huge amount of discipline to keep focused on the discussion of the takeover when his mind wanted to drift to thoughts of Caroline Duplessis. The only information he had on her was the brief fact sheet his staff had assembled while investigating Laurel. Of course, he would have a full dossier by the end of the day, but the deal had already been put on the table, and he was a man of his word. His impulsive offer was not the way he did business-ever.

But every nerve ending and synapse had demanded he ask her to marry him. So he had. He was still stunned that she had accepted.

Enough pondering. He had work to do. "Mrs. Willoughby, start a full background check on Miss Duplessis, please. Everything from grade school detentions to shoe size."

His call to Jack would mean no turning back. "Jack," he spoke into the phone, "can you break away from whatever you're doing and come up to draft another prenuptial agreement?"

"Sure. I've got a free spot on my calendar this afternoon. Have you had a chance to look over the list? Anyone you want my staff to set up with an interview?"

"No. That won't be necessary. I've already made my choice and she's accepted."

"That was fast. Who?"

"Caroline Duplessis, Laurel's wedding planner."

"She wasn't on the list." Jack shuffled papers on his end. "We ran a preliminary background check on her when Laurel hired her. Petite? Quiet? Reserved?"

"That's the one."

"Not your type at all. How did that happen?"

Unexplainable words like happenstance and fate popped into Brandon's thoughts. "Not important. Just bring the boilerplate contract and be ready to make some changes to it."

As he broke the connection, Mrs. Willoughby knocked on his door.

"Enter."

She had a slim file folder in her hands and a sour expression on her face. "Here's the information you wanted. Not much to it, so it was easy to find." She dropped Caroline's file onto his desk with more attitude than necessary.

"Do you have something to say to me, Mrs. Willoughby?"

"I have plenty to say, but nothing you'll want to hear." She planted her feet and crossed her arms, clearly not intending to leave any time soon.

"You know I value your opinions." Brandon also knew the sooner his secretary had her say, the sooner her unruffled disposition would return.

"It's none of my business what you do in your personal life. But I've known you for many years. You're a good man. You deserve a good woman." She uncrossed her arms and picked up a dead leaf from the plant she watered each Wednesday. "If you would take the time to enjoy life, meet nice people, laugh and have fun, Brandon, you would become the man you're meant to be."

Before Brandon could respond, she skimmed up two more dead leaves and left his office.

The man he was meant to be. According to his mother, he wasn't meant to be, at all. He was an accident that should have never happened. An accident that had ruined her life. He would never let a moment of irresponsible lust ruin anyone else's life, ever again.

He might have picked Caroline on instinct, but the rest of their relationship would be carefully planned and executed, and she would be no worse for her experience when their agreement concluded. In fact, he was willing to make sure she was much better off for having married him. He planned to be very generous with his money. *As long as she didn't try to get personal.*

His self-reflection was mercifully interrupted when Jack rapped on the door, signature enthusiasm coming through in the rhythm of his knock.

An hour later, Jack was no longer so enthusiastic.

"This contract goes beyond tight. It's downright insulting. I don't like having my firm's name attached to it. Why would anyone want to marry you after reading this?"

Brandon stood and looked out his window at the crowd below, his back to Jack. "Money. Why does anyone do anything? It all comes down to money."

Jack scraped his chair as he stood. "It's a bit early, but I think I need a drink to wash this bad taste from my mouth."

Brandon watched him go, wondering himself why he had insisted on the unique clauses and particular wording in this prenuptial contract. He hadn't expected so much from Laurel. Why was Caroline so different?

Caroline drove under the canopy of live oaks that lined the streets of the Garden District past houses that had been passed down from father to son since New Orleans was founded.

More than once, panic had threatened to take her breath away. She would pick up the phone to beg off the agreement but, using all her willpower, would make her fingers dial another creditor to beg for a little more time to pay off her debts, instead. While placing all those phone calls, though, she never found the courage to call her parents and break the nuptial news to them.

She pulled up in front of a New Orleans version of neoclassical architecture and checked the address. Yes, right house, although she would hardly call this a house. The mansion was larger than some hotels she'd stayed in.

Across the street, a Greek Revival competed for attention. The lavish landscaping made the Greek Revival appear well loved as well as well financed. Ferns in large urns softened the columns. Pots of brightly colored annuals lined the walkway.

Comparatively, Brandon's home could use some personal touches. The wrought iron fencing surrounding the estate was freshly painted black. Shrubbery was precisely trimmed, and the lawn was meticulously groomed, but no splashes of color welcomed guests. The whole front garden was austere, just like its owner.

She didn't fit here.

Nervously, she rubbed her bare arms, suddenly chilled despite the Louisiana heat. Instead of the flouncy sundress she had chosen, she should have worn a formal business jacket and skirt. This wasn't a date, after all. Too late to worry about that now.

As she exited her car, she saw movement on the veranda and squinted through the falling dusk. Brandon wore a polo shirt in rich burgundy that stretched across his chest and draped across his flat stomach. His jeans hugged his hips and thighs, and his belt and shoes looked lived in, the kind of lived in that could only be purchased in the highest of upper-end designer departments.

He came down the deep steps fronting his home to meet her. His confident saunter said king of his castle more blatantly than a crown and scepter.

"Welcome." He held out his hand.

"Thank you." She put her hand in his, expecting a polite shake. Instead, he carried it to his lips for the briefest of social kisses. No doubt about it, he was old-school Creole. While he was only being polite, she couldn't help that her heart sped up at the brush of his lips on her sensitive skin.

When one of her heels wedged in the brick walkway, she stumbled.

He immediately caught her hand and tucked it close into the crook of his elbow. "Careful. These are the original cobblestones, and they've shifted in the last few centuries."

The veranda stretched the length of the house, wide enough to hold a party of seventy-five with ease. In the dimming light, she saw that the cool grey paint was fresh. Light from inside glowed through the stained glass on the double front doors and sidelights. While it was all grandiose, it also looked...lonely.

In Caroline's imagination, she could envision wicker rocking chairs and occasional tables holding mint juleps while fern fronds waved from hanging baskets along the roof's edge.

This veranda was made for laughter and the patter of

little feet. She started up the wide stairs before her thoughts could run any farther down that path.

Brandon opened one of the two massive double doors and ushered her into a hallway as wide as most rooms.

"How beautiful!" Caroline admired the Grande Hall in all its glory. It stretched forever with intricate moldings framing the ceiling and massive doorways opening into the other rooms. Construction paraphernalia sat at the far end of the hall, a testament to ongoing work.

"Restoration is almost complete." Pride revealed itself in the square set of Brandon's shoulders, even if his voice remained noncommittal.

He snagged a pair of crystal wine glasses from a japanned tray and handed one to her.

"Thank you." Caroline sipped, enjoying the cold fruity taste. She rarely drank. Alcohol went to her head so fast. But tonight was a unique occasion, and she would stop in plenty of time before her drive home.

Caroline pointed to the Aubusson rugs that cushioned her feet from the polished oak flooring. "These are in great condition. They can't be real."

"I had them woven to match the originals." He swept his arm to include the wallpaper, wall sconces, and huge chandeliers overhead. "My decorator has strict instructions to stay as close to the original colors and patterns as possible. I've been lucky. She's found many of the original furnishings in the upstairs attics."

Brandon put his hand in the small of her back to gently guide her down the hallway, more evidence of his classic manners. The masculine gesture made her feel cherished for her femininity. There was no question in her mind why he was on the top of the Most Eligible list.

"I've been restoring her ever since I got her back."

"Got her back?" Caroline peeked into a drawing room

restored to perfection using a rose palette. An antique pianoforte stood near the fireplace while graceful chairs sat in a comfortable semicircle nearby.

"My grandfather won this house from his cousin in a card game during the Great Depression. Personally, I think the owner lost it on purpose. The house came with several years of back taxes that my grandfather had to pay off."

"At least it stayed in the family."

"For a while." Brandon stopped before the open entrance of the other drawing room. Caroline winced at the orange-and-brown flowered vinyl paper on the walls, the drop lighting and the acrylic shag carpet on the floor.

"What happened here?"

"Awful, isn't it?" Brandon squinted as if the colors hurt his eyes. "A house like this takes a lot of upkeep, and my father's ventures weren't always successful. He sold it after my grandparents passed it to him. That's when *this* happened."

"When did you buy it back?"

"I didn't actually buy it."

"I don't understand."

"In keeping with my grandfather's tradition, I won it in a hand of five card draw." His sincere smile showed the hint of the dimple in his left cheek. "Again, the owner owed quite a sum in back taxes."

"Who is doing the restoration?"

"Stafford House."

Caroline mentally increased her estimate of the restoration by twenty percent. "You must have won it back a while ago. I understand that Stafford House has a five-year waiting list."

"I think they usually do. But patience isn't one of my virtues. They were happy to make other arrangements when offered a monetary incentive."

In addition to being a stickler for detail, her future

husband obviously didn't mind paying for what he wanted.

Future husband. She felt her knees go weak. *Six months, Caroline. You can do anything for six months*, she reminded herself. And you might as well make the best of it.

"Careful." Noting her open-toed heels, Brandon spread his hand protectively on her waist to usher her past construction debris down the hallway.

No since in resisting. She'd already agreed to the arrangement, and she would do her part to make it work. She let herself lean into his touch.

He led her into a kitchen worthy of any boutique restaurant. "Instead of restoring the kitchen, I added on and updated."

Chrome appliances, cool tile, and marble countertops were warmed by mellow oak cabinets.

"Oh, Brandon, this is magnificent!"

"You cook?"

"Some. Mostly basics." She ran her hand across the smooth marble. "I've always wanted to explore the art of Creole and Cajun cooking."

Almost hesitantly, he said, "I don't mind your experimenting on me."

For what he was paying her, she could certainly whip up a few meals. "It's a deal."

He pointed to an open bottle of white wine chilling in a bucket on the counter. "More?"

She held her glass out for a refill and raised it to toast. "To us."

"To us," he echoed back.

The small exchange made her glow. This arrangement—she hadn't been able to call it a marriage yet, even in her own thoughts—might work out all right.

Bolstered by the camaraderie and the wine, Caroline asked the question that had been burning within her ever since her arrival.

"Where are the bedrooms?" She couldn't hold back the blush as she asked. The ensuing silence made her feel awkward and gawky.

"Upstairs, but mine is the only one finished—"

"I won't sleep with you," she blurted out. "I don't even know you."

It seemed she had used up her daily supply of grace and poise. Mortified at her gauche outburst, Caroline wanted to turn tail and run, but her shocked body wouldn't make a move.

Surprise darted across Brandon's eyes before flatness took over. It was the same flatness that Caroline had seen in the video. "I don't recall issuing the invitation."

Caroline hadn't meant to be so tactless. She had meant to approach the subject more delicately. But now that it was done—

"I just wanted to lay my cards on the table upfront," she mumbled. While she was glad she had the whole topic behind her, a niggling disappointment at his immediate rejection tickled the back of her mind. What was wrong with her that he wouldn't want her?

"Poker vernacular, Caroline? There's quite a bit I don't know about you." Brandon gave her a thorough look over. "Why don't we talk about it while we take a look at the prenuptial contract? Come into my study."

The old nursery rhyme that began "Come into my parlor, said the spider to the fly" popped into Caroline's mind.

Brandon turned on his heel and headed back down the hallway, leaving Caroline to follow him. As she walked behind, she felt a chill where his hand had been.

But then, there was no room for warmth in a business arrangement. With her intentions firmly back in place, Caroline followed behind him.

He ushered her into a lush office larger than her whole

apartment with burgundy leather chairs, two matching black walnut desks, each with streamlined computer monitors and bookcases lining the walls. Leaded-glass clerestory windows set high in the outside walls brought light into a room that otherwise tended toward darkness. "I had this room added with technological communication in mind. I think the architect did a good job of blending in with the original construction."

Caroline studied the room that lacked all signs of personalization. Not even a snapshot in a picture frame to grace the shelves. "I would never have guessed this room wasn't original to the house."

"Please, have a seat." Brandon gestured to a Louis XV guest chair across from one of the desks. While the chair wasn't as short as the one in his riverfront office, setting it opposite the massive desk effectively served the same purpose of putting a visitor in her place.

Brandon seated himself behind the desk, picked up his glasses, and reached into a drawer to pull out a sheaf of papers.

He handed over a dozen pages to her. "This is the background check on you. Is there anything inaccurate or that I need to add?"

"You had me investigated?"

"I have all my business partners investigated. Nothing personal."

"Nothing personal," Caroline repeated. It certainly felt personal when her life was reduced to a folder full of papers she could hold in one hand. "Just business."

Quickly scanning, Caroline saw the report was both accurate and thorough.

"I noticed your father is a renowned academic and your parents are spending the summer in Minnesota where your father will guest lecture for the Mathematics Department at the local university," Brandon commented. "You must get your entrepreneurship from your mother."

The papers listed her mother's various business ventures, which included a bookstore, a hat shop, and a tourist mart as well as her bridal gown business.

Her father's academic journey up the ivory tower was catalogued as well. On the last page, Caroline found a complete workup of her finances. Brandon's report showed the numbers to be even bleaker than her own calculations.

"Seeing my life reduced to a few pages makes me feel rather boring and insignificant."

"Your small file speaks of your virtuousness. All you've got against you is debt, and that's common enough. Nefariousness makes for a much thicker file. So, in this case, boring is a good thing."

Caroline thought of all the tabloid stories Brandon had been featured in. The playboy image might not be accurate, but the ruthless negotiator was right on key.

She understood his reminder of her debt, seeing it for what it was, a reminder that she needed to go through with this arrangement, regardless of second thoughts she might be having.

"Speaking of virtue—" He looked at her over the rims of his glasses. "You wanted to discuss our sleeping arrangements?"

Yes, he knew how to pick his moments to his best advantage. She would not want to be on the receiving end of a hostile negotiation.

She gulped her wine. "Yes, please."

He pinned her with his total attention waiting-daring?-her to speak up. Would he have the same intensity in bed?

"I have a penthouse above my office where I usually sleep."

She cleared her throat. "That could be a problem."

"Oh?"

How could he do that? How could he make the coldness in his eyes come and go at will? Caroline felt herself wanting to bring the warmth back as quickly as possible.

Despite her best intentions, she felt herself blushing again. She squared her shoulders and forced herself to meet his powerful gaze. "It would break my parents' hearts to think that I'm marrying you for any reason other than deep and abiding love. They mustn't know this is purely a business deal. If you sleep in your penthouse while I sleep here, the tabloids would find out, no matter how discreet we are. My mother loves the celebrity magazines."

Brandon relaxed, and Caroline felt like the mouse who had just pulled the thorn from the lion's paw. "Not a problem. We'll be pretending to be madly in love to the rest of the world. We'll just keep up the pretense around your family, too. The mistress's bedroom is almost complete. I'll have the workmen finish it by tomorrow night. Does that put your mind at ease?"

Caroline let her shoulders slump in relief. At least she told herself it was relief. Why, then, had she felt a fleeting moment of anticipation followed by disappointment before her mind took over from her emotions?

"Yes. Fine. Thank you."

"Do I hear some hesitation there?" Brandon's voice deepened, making her heart throb. "I pride myself on making sure my partners are completely satisfied."

She caught herself leaning closer. His pupils darkened, and Caroline was sure they were both thinking of the same type of satisfaction. She had the most deliciously wicked image of herself reaching across the desk, taking off his glasses, and discovering the Superman behind the business persona.

The gong of the grandfather clock in the hallway broke into her thoughts, and Brandon glanced at his watch. "It's getting late. Shall we get on with the contract?"

Caroline found herself blinking as if she were coming out of a trance. What was it about this man that was so mesmerizing? And why didn't she want to be immune to his allure?

Brandon handed her a thick document. "I'll attend to a few emails while you read over the contract."

Brandon refilled her glass, and Caroline sipped as she read.

Being a wedding planner, Caroline had seen more than one prenuptial agreement, so she was primed to expect anything.

The legalese was right upfront about the amount of alimony granted her should the marriage end after six months. A longer marriage meant a proportionately larger alimony settlement.

She only paused a second when she read the conditions of undesirable behavior that could make the agreement null and void. Since Caroline had no intention of posing nude for public or private distribution, nor was she prone to acting without decorum at any public or private gathering, the requirements didn't concern her. She did appreciate that Brandon had added an exception to the decorum clause for football games where emotional outbursts were perfectly acceptable.

The conception clause was a different matter. Brandon insisted on proof that she was not pregnant before the prenuptial contract would be binding. Caroline would take all measures to ensure that pregnancy did not occur while they were married. Caroline read the next paragraph three times, to make sure she understood.

Should she become pregnant or have a child while they were married "wife agrees to undergo and/or allow child to undergo testing to verify paternity of child. Should the husband named in this agreement be father of said child, wife agrees to relinquish custody *in parentis* and *in loco*. The wife further agrees that no child support or alimony will be due upon the dissolution of the marriage."

While she should have expected a clause like this from a man with a reputation as ruthless as Brandon's, Caroline couldn't help but take offense. She had to take another peek at the money to calm herself. Knowing she would be debt free in six months did much to strengthen her resolve.

She swallowed down the last of her wine, clearing the sour taste from her mouth.

Of course, avoiding this clause would not be a problem. First, there were the birth control pills she took to regulate her periods. Second, and more definitively, there was the fact that she was a virgin and had no intention of changing that state during the next six months, regardless of any attraction she might feel toward Brandon.

She had waited this long for the perfect man to come along. She wouldn't throw away all her restraint for a short-term business arrangement.

Involuntarily, Caroline found herself staring at Brandon as he studied his computer screen. What kind of lover would he be? Thorough, for sure. Impatient, but holding back so the timing was perfect. He'd said it himself, he prided himself on making sure his partner was satisfied.

Brandon must have felt her gaze upon him because he looked up. "Yes?"

She pointed to the complicated signature lines for witnesses and notary seals. Her tongue felt thick as she said, "I'll sign whenever you're ready."

"Excellent. We'll have it witnessed and filed right away."

"About the wedding." Caroline dug into her purse and pulled out her calendar. "I think I can arrange a simple ceremony by Saturday after next."

"No need." Brandon took off his glasses. "We're getting

married tonight."

Chapter Five

Tonight?" Caroline whispered as all color drained from her face.

Brandon stood and came around his desk, then knelt by her chair, ready to push her head down below her heart to revive her should she faint. But she was made of sterner stuff.

"I'm a wedding planner. I know the marriage laws of Louisiana. We must wait seventy-two hours after we obtain our marriage license." Temper flared as she looked him in the eye. "What's your game here?"

He had never knelt at a woman's feet before. Now, as he did so, he was certain he didn't like the position, especially when the woman was extremely angry.

But her flare of passion totally turned him on. He had wanted her ever since she entered his office, although he still couldn't put reason to it. Now, her show of inner fire made him want her even more. Who would have guessed so much passion lurked behind her reserved façade?

"So you're not going to faint?"

"I never faint." Her eyes glistened, turning them into the multifaceted amber of a feline. Her breasts rose and fell with each breath. Her body radiated electricity.

He wanted to touch her for the joy of the spark. Instead, he put his fingers on the chair's armrest, inches from her fingertips. She twitched, then moved her hand away as if she felt that energy between them, too. He'd bet the bank that she had.

"Good to know." He stood, regretting the distance between them.

What was it about this woman that broke through his shell of jadedness? Was it her cool surface that hid glimpses of blazing emotions? Was it her determination to meet him as an equal when so many bowed and scraped to him?

Whatever it was, he wanted it. He wanted her.

"I filled out the paperwork for the license this afternoon. Since marriage licenses are public record, the world will know tomorrow who you are and that we're getting married. Delaying the wedding will only give the media vultures a chance to exploit the wedding."

She twirled her empty wine glass. "What about the three-day wait?"

"A judge can waive that requirement."

"And you know a judge, of course."

"I made a call. He's across the street with my attorney, waiting."

She stiffened and sat up straight, affront in every line. "They're watching us from across the street? Spying on us?"

"Nothing quite so dramatic. My lawyer owns the Greek Revival you admired when you arrived. The judge frequently plays poker with us. He has agreed to witness our contract and marry us." Brandon held up the wine bottle, and she waved it off.

"What if I hadn't agreed to your terms? You were taking quite a risk that I'd say yes, weren't you?"

"Taking risks is what I do. And reading people is what I

do best."

"How do you read me now?" In her anger, her voice was raw with emotion and utterly sexy. She leaned toward him, her breath coming faster than normal, her color high in each check, her eyes glistening.

This is how she will look right before she comes for me.

She had said no sex, and he respected that. But he had seen the way she looked at him when he was scanning through his e-mail, as if she'd like to eat him for dessert.

It was a woman's prerogative to change her mind and a man's right to convince her to change it. Brandon prided himself on getting what he wanted, and he wanted her.

He had six months to seduce her into his bed, but he'd already explained he wasn't a patient man. He knew how to make his world move on a faster track. If he were to wager, he would place his bet on one month, max.

The challenge made him ache for her.

His body responded to hers as his pulse rate ratcheted even higher.

Standing, he leaned against the edge of his desk and swallowed against his reaction to her nipples that had peaked under the thin fabric of her sundress. A slip of material was all that separated them from his mouth. Her lips parted, and she scraped her bottom lip with her teeth. Her pupils expanded, making it so easy to fall into those eyes. Yes, she felt it, too.

His heart pounded in his chest. He had to look away to gather his thoughts. No woman had ever had this effect on him before.

Mentally, he adjusted his bet. Two weeks. Two weeks might be all he could bear.

He swallowed the last of his wine as he wished for whiskey instead. Following desires with actions, he walked over to his sideboard and poured himself a measure. Giving himself time to rein in his more carnal desires, he studied his glass before taking a long, slow sip. *Control, Brandon. Control. This is purely business.*

Willing logic to conquer lust, he said, "I read you as a sensible woman who knows that delaying our marriage will only make our lives more complicated."

She calmed as his reasoning sunk in. Her eyes settled back to deep, tranquil amber, and she sat back in her chair, once again unruffled on the surface.

The whole passion-infused exchange couldn't have taken but a few minutes, but it seemed like a lifetime to Brandon. Knowing he'd seen a rare glimpse of what she hid beneath that composed exterior made her more fascinating by the second.

"Upstairs in the master bath, you'll find a home pregnancy test under the sink."

Visibly, she swallowed down her first response and said instead, "You're fairly sure the results will be negative, aren't you?"

"Yes. Pregnant women have a certain look." An image of Caroline heavy with his child invaded his thoughts, but he quickly suppressed it. Children were not in his future. Not now. Not ever. "But it's best for both of us if we fulfill the terms of the contract to the letter. Loopholes only cause confusion."

"Yes. Of course. I understand. Nothing personal. Just business." With great deliberateness, Caroline stood and exited the room showing Brandon a spine so rigid he was certain she would break before she would bend.

For the first time in his life, Brandon wished it were more than just business. He stuffed his foolishness safely back in that mental box with all his other hard-learned lessons and dialed Jack's number.

"Jack, it's time. Bring the judge." He barked, as soon as he heard the click of the phone being picked up.

"Hello? Please? Thank you? Have you forgotten the

manners your momma taught you?" The woman who answered the phone certainly wasn't Jack.

Brandon was positive he called the right number. "You are...?"

"Jack's neighbor," she answered. "And you are--?"

"Also his neighbor."

"Ah. Then please hold, neighbor, while I get Mr. Sumrall."

Why was a strange woman at Jack's house now? Jack knew how crucial secrecy and timing were for this deal to go through.

She'd said she was a neighbor. The house next to Jack had been turned into a quadplex and donated to some kind of starving-artist society. Strange people moved in and out all the time. And Brandon meant *strange* quite emphatically. But why would one of them be in Jack's house along with the judge?

He trusted Jack—usually. Had feminine wiles corrupted Jack's judgment? Women were certainly the downfall of plenty of good men. As strong-willed as Jack was, Brandon had always figured that Jack was immune, like he was. Brandon hadn't been wrong in a while. Perhaps he was due.

"Sumrall, here." Jack identified himself without this usual Southern drawl. Something was definitely wrong at Jack's house. He never lost his equanimity. By the sharpness of his voice, his visitor must be an unwelcomed one.

"Everything went as planned. It's time."

"You'll be having a guest. My neighbor, Ursula. The judge invited her to share your happy occasion." Jack's tone changed to forced joviality. "The judge is greatly taken with Ursula." In a quieter voice, he added, "Your press release is ready to go, so she can't scoop the official news. I don't think she's that type anyway."

"Just what type is she?"

"I'm not sure." Jack sounded frustrated and confused,

totally out of character. "But she insists on attending the wedding."

"Fine. Let's get this over with." At the sound of a sharply indrawn breath, Brandon looked up and saw Caroline standing in his doorway. "I've got to go. Come over. Now."

Hearing the cold hard way Brandon regarded their marriage, Caroline had to reach deep inside herself to gather the remnants of her self-respect around her. This was a business arrangement, a merger of expedience and nothing else. "The evidence is on the sink. You'll find everything as I said. I'll wait here while you examine it."

Brandon nodded and headed for the stairs. For a fleeting second, she thought he would trust her. But trust hadn't built his financial empire, and trust wasn't what their marriage was based upon. Contractual agreements tied Brandon D'Estrehan's world together.

The doorbell rang, and Caroline debated answering it. This was not her home, after all. But it soon would be. She might as well begin the way she meant to go on.

She could do this. She could be a gracious hostess, an arm ornament, a token wife. She could do anything for six months to be debt free and keep her parents' home intact. Her time with Brandon didn't have to be difficult. The terms were the same whether she enjoyed her time under contract or not.

Two men in casual office attire and a lovely young woman in a tie-dyed halter dress carrying a huge bouquet of flowers stood before her.

"Welcome." She gestured them into the Grande Hall, frowning as her words came out a little thick. She'd thought she'd been handling her nerves rather well.

"Congratulations." The woman hugged her, flowers and all. "I'm Ursula. Thank you for allowing me to share in your happiness."

"Judge Riley, my dear." The judge also gave her a hug, a

bit more familiar than she felt comfortable with. He smelled of cologne and cocktails. She moved away, putting distance between them. But distancing herself didn't impede the judge's overfriendliness.

"So you're Brandon's bride. You must be quite a woman to capture our young man so shortly after——." He stopped himself just shy of mentioning the called-off wedding as Brandon entered the hall.

He had changed into a pair of dark slacks and a white button-down with a casual jacket, a perfect complement to her sundress. The look played up his confident allure as well as his intense coloring. He came toward them, his attention anchored on her.

Caroline's senses prickled as she found herself staring. Everything about the man captivated her. Even his walk shouted of charisma.

Brandon caught her and pulled her to him, putting his arm around her shoulders. "What were you saying, Judge? I didn't catch the end of it."

Caroline felt safe and sheltered from the judge's probing. Today had been such a long day. The longest and fastest of her life. For just a second, she allowed herself to lean into Brandon's strength.

The judge stole a sideways glance at Caroline before answering Brandon. "Just extending my best wishes, of course."

Brandon's arm tightened protectively. His face looked fierce, warrior-like, as if he would shield her from the world. "Caroline is a very special lady, Judge."

"Anyone can see they're crazy for each other, can't they, Jack?" Ursula broke in. "Can't you feel the passion in their vibes?"

Apparently, words failed Jack, a rarity in a lawyer. Under Ursula's scrutiny, he nodded his agreement.

Satisfied, she handed the bouquet to Caroline. "Jack mentioned that this is a spontaneous wedding. The best kind, in my opinion. No posturing for other people's benefits, just pure love for each other. You two are made for each other." She winked. "I have the gift for knowing these types of things."

Jack suddenly found his voice. "Let's get the papers signed and get on with it, then. Your office, Brandon?"

"Yes. And the wedding will take place in the front drawing room. If your friend—" he looked pointedly from Jack to Ursula and back again, "—would wait for us in there."

"Sure," Ursula bubbled. "This is all so romantic, isn't it?"

In Brandon's office, Jack produced two identical copies of the contract Caroline had read earlier. He flipped them all to the back pages, keeping the contents safe from judging eyes.

"Sign here, here, and here." He pointed to the blank lines. "And sign the wedding license here."

The judge and Jack served as witnesses, and then it was legal. The rest was simply a formality to seal the deal.

All of a sudden, the reality hit Caroline. She was about to do this. She was really, truly about to marry a man she had only met that day.

Without conscious thought, Caroline stopped walking. Once stopped, she couldn't find the will to continue. Her feet refused to take another step forward. She felt as if her entire world had begun to spin.

Brandon rested his hand on her back, and the spinning slowed. He leaned close and whispered so that only she could hear, "Are you all right?"

"I'm not sure," she admitted. "I'm a bit dizzy."

Brandon ordered the judge and Jack to go ahead. "We'll join you in a minute."

He poured her a brandy from a decanter next to his whiskey. "Drink."

The brandy was smooth, too smooth. Caroline drank it down faster than she should have. The liquid bravado did its job, settling her nerves but leaving her world soft and fuzzy.

"I'm ready."

"Excellent. Let's go." He held out his hand to her.

Caroline blinked twice, but all the crisp lines in his palm had blurred. In fact, everything was blurred.

As Caroline tried to focus, she realized she hadn't eaten since breakfast. Brandon D'Estrehan had kept her too on edge to eat. And she was about to marry the man.

She took another deep drink. The warmth of the brandy kept spreading and spreading, numbing reality more and more. Now she was ready.

"Uh-oh. I'm not sure I can stand."

He looped her arm through his and helped her up. "Lean on me. I won't let you fall."

"I believe you. You'll always catch me, won't you?" She felt a loose smile curve her lips. They, too, felt soft and fuzzy.

"Yes, always."

"Too much, too fast." She touched her mouth with her finger.

"I'll make it up to you."

"Promise? Cross your heart?"

"Cross my heart, promise."

She blinked through the fog. "Are you patronizing me?"

"Yes, absolutely."

"Smart man." She patted the hand that held firmly to her arm. "My flowers. Where are my flowers?"

Without letting her go, he snagged her bouquet from the desk.

She took the huge colorful arrangement of zinnias and daisies in both hands, keeping her arm looped through his. "These are supposed to be magnolia blossoms."

"Not roses?"

"No. Roses have thorns." A wave of sadness brought a flicker of soberness. "I'm ready."

As if in a dream, Caroline found herself facing the judge. Ursula played the pianoforte, a light aria that trilled up and down the scale. Candles flickered on the mantle, and the judge took his place with his back to the unlit fireplace.

Caroline leaned into Brandon as he stood firm holding her against him through their linked arms. The bouquet hid her shaking hands.

When Ursula finished, she joined Caroline. Jack stepped up next to Brandon. Caroline couldn't have arranged their placements any better herself.

If only her parents were here…. But then, that would seem too much like a real wedding.

The judge read the traditional ceremony, stumbling over her last name, which Jack stage-whispered to him. Caroline learned her husband-to-be's middle name was Andrew.

She swayed, and Brandon moved closer to wrap his arm around her waist. When prompted, Caroline said, "I do" and "I will." Her throat felt raw, as if she'd been crying.

Strength surged through her when she heard Brandon's baritone answering the same, but a moment of loss swept through her when Brandon released her. When Ursula reached for her bouquet, she handed it over and wrung her fingers until Brandon asked for her hand.

At his touch, warmth spread from fingertips to wrist, up her arm, to her heart.

He put a heavy antique ring on her finger. The ring was too big, and the citrine stone slid around to her palm. Despite the fit, she loved the feel. How many generations had worn this ring before her?

She sighed. She would have to give it back when this was all over. While technically she might have a claim on the ring, giving it up would be the right thing to do.

Ursula nudged her and gave her a man's ring, a simple gold band. Caroline took Brandon's hand and concentrated on lining up the ring with his finger. The fit was snugly perfect. But then, the ring had been made for him for that other wedding that never happened.

Caroline traced the gold with her finger. She knew she should let him have his hand back, but she didn't want to turn him loose.

The judge said, "You may kiss the bride."

Brandon leaned in close and looked into Caroline's eyes. Just a few more millimeters and their lips would touch. Time stood still.

Nervous, she licked her lips.

For the first time in her life, Caroline had no idea what came next. What would her days be like after this kiss?

Thinking that hard started to clear her head so she pushed away her worries.

For this moment in time, she would enjoy what life put in front of her. The future was in the future.

Brandon's mouth took possession of hers, and she surrendered willingly, falling, falling, falling into wedded bliss.

Chapter Six

Caroline woke to the feel of cool, fresh sheets caressing her naked body.

Naked? She had never, ever slept naked. Having nothing between her and the open air but a layer of fine cotton made her skin prickle with awareness.

Prying her eyes open made the throb in her skull more than a hazy dream. Sunlight streamed in the window. Squinting against the bright beams didn't help her headache at all.

Nor did sitting up quickly when she realized she was not in her bed. Then she remembered—at least part of last night.

As if it were all a watercolor painting, she remembered vague outlines and impressions; signing the contract, saying "I do", agreeing with the judge that Ursula made the best hurricanes in the South, kissing Brandon.

Oh, did she ever remember kissing Brandon! Her nipples peaked, already responsive to the smooth cotton sheets rubbing against them. The sensation was excruciatingly lovely.

Why was she so aroused this morning? She didn't remember removing her dress. Had Brandon...?

Just what had Brandon done?

Was that whispery tickle on the nape of her neck a dream or a memory? How about the caress down her spine or the hand skimming her shoulders and then her hip bone?

She wasn't sore where virgins were supposed to be sore. Wouldn't she know if she were no longer a virgin? Of course, she would.

But what other liberties had her husband taken? What other liberties had she allowed? Moaned for? She distinctly remembered sighing as Brandon stroked her skin. Or had he touched her at all? She wished she could think through the haze that enshrouded her brain. Wished she could remember clearly. *Wished Brandon were lying next to her.*

What? What had she just wished for? Caroline sat up—too quickly—as the bed seemed to heave and roll beneath her. She clutched the sheets and drew them up over her breasts, knowing it was too little, too late.

The quietness of the house gave her a hint that Brandon had already left for the day. But then, it was a big house. She might not hear him.

She could tell he had been there, though. In the bed next to her. His scent lingered on the pillow next to her. No note, though. But then, this wasn't a movie. It was real life, for better or worse until she met the terms of the prenuptial contract.

On the nightstand, her phone vibrated. She snagged it and blinked to see the display. Half past ten and a tiny pulsating message icon.

The last time she'd slept so late, she'd had the flu. Her head hadn't hurt nearly as badly then as now. Also on the bedside table was a glass of water and a fizzy antacid tablet. As far as gifts went, it was the best one she had ever received.

She tore the packet with her teeth, regretting the jarring but unable to tear it with her fingers. While it fizzed in the water, she dialed voice mail.

The robotic voice cheerfully informed her that she had

twenty-three messages. A couple of buttons showed her another seventeen text messages waiting to be read.

Ignoring all the electronic annoyances, she downed half the antacid in one swallow, then breathed carefully and shallowly to make sure it stayed where she had put it before sipping the rest of the glass down.

With curative in place, she tackled her voice messages. The first one in the queue was from Brandon. "The workmen are holding off until you give them the okay. When you wake up, call the foreman so they can get back on the job."

"And a good morning to you, too," she muttered as she saved the message for later.

The next message was from her mother. "Caroline? Your father and I saw you on one of those celebrity expose shows last night. What is going on? Your father and I are very worried. Call us."

Her stomach revolted at that one.

Then a call from Paula. "So you're the reason for the called-off wedding. I knew you sounded guarded yesterday. What happened, Caroline? The girls are saying all kinds of awful things about you." Paula's message paused, and Caroline heard a muffled background conversation. "Call me with the straight scoop, and I'll do what I can to set the record straight. There's a reporter who wants to talk to me. He seems like he'll listen to reason. I just need to know what to tell him."

Oh, no! Caroline hadn't even thought about people seeing her in that way. And this was supposed to be a love match, so what could she say? She certainly couldn't tell anyone the truth.

She paged through the next messages, many from reporters. How they had gotten her cell phone number, she couldn't guess. The others were just variations and repeats from her mother, her father, and Paula.

Except the last one in the queue. Mrs. Willoughby.

"Good morning, Mrs. D'Estrehan. It seems congratulations are in order. Mr. D'Estrehan has made arrangements for your personal items to be retrieved from your apartment at your convenience. And he has scheduled a briefing with his public relations specialist at his office at noon. A light luncheon will be served. He has arranged a car and a driver for your convenience as the next few days may be a bit hectic." Mrs. Willoughby rattled off the company name and number of the driver, although it sounded more like a security firm than a car service.

Her phone buzzed with another message. Brandon?

The caller ID showed her Paula's number again, so she ignored it. An aloneness she'd never felt before swamped her.

Wouldn't most women be anxious to talk to their best friends? She and Paula had been friends since childhood, along with a handful of other girls. She was the quiet one of the group, the one that remembered to tip the waiter and volunteered to be the designated driver—a wisdom she'd blithely abandoned last night.

As she thought about it, she realized she hung with them out of habit. While they shared their innermost secrets, she had never felt safe telling them about her deepest desire for a happily ever after or the financial struggles of starting her own business. She was the listener, not the talker. And now that she wanted to talk, Paula wanted to sell her story to a gossip magazine.

She wanted to curl back into a ball and sleep, but she had an appointment with her new husband and the clock was ticking.

Her sundress lay over the bedroom chair, so wrinkled it looked like she had slept in it. But if she had, she wouldn't be sitting naked in Brandon's bed clutching the sheet to her neck.

A hazy memory peeked around the corner of her dulling headache, more impressions and feelings than concrete recall.

The built-in bra in the tight bodice biting into her, the fitted waist twisting, cutting off her air. Then panic and a struggle, her own as she tried to grasp the zipper and breathe. Strong hands rescued her as Brandon worked the zipper free. He had helped her shrug the dress from her shoulders and disentangle the full skirt from her legs.

Then what happened?

Try as she might, she couldn't remember. The next moment of lucidity she'd had was when she opened her eyes this morning.

She needed a shower. Hopefully, the rushing water would sluice away her fog so she could make sense of what she had done.

Bleary-eyed, Brandon checked his e-mail and sipped the strongest chicory coffee he had ever attempted to drink. No doubt about it, last night was the longest night of his life.

Who would have guessed that while Caroline quietly nursed her drink in the corner, she was getting totally soused?

The judge had insisted that Ursula demonstrate her bartending skills, and the rounds of toasts had followed. It seemed that Ursula had taken his little bride under her wing and was determined to make a large celebration out of the miniscule wedding party. They stayed for hours, toasting and talking and even insisting on a wedding waltz. The dance happened while Caroline was still standing.

After the guests left, he had planned to surreptitiously take Caroline back to her apartment, but there was no way he could have just dropped her off at her door when she was semiconscious at best. So he had carried her up to his room and put her in his bed.

He would have left her there except for her outflung hand and pitiful moan of "Don't leave me." He should have left her. He should have turned around right then and there and headed for his too-short couch in his office.

Instead, he climbed into bed with her. He would have had to have the discipline of a saint to resist tracing her ankle when he took off her shoes. Or touching her bare back where her sundress dipped low. Or leaning in to taste the sweetness of the nape of her neck.

Nobody had ever accused him of sainthood.

But then she started struggling with her dress, begging him to take it off. Of course, he did.

He had expected some reciprocity. Instead, he'd received a kitten-like snore.

Frustration raged through him.

The midnight run hadn't given him any relief. Neither had the cold shower or the drive to the office in the predawn hours. In fact, this was shaping up to be the most torturous twelve hours he'd ever had.

And now Caroline wouldn't answer her phone. Was she really sleeping this late, or was she ignoring him?

He dialed her cell phone for the third time that morning. When he heard the voice mail message, he disconnected, again. He would give her ten more minutes and then he would send the car to check on her.

The cleanup did its job. Caroline could now think clearly on the consequences of yesterday's actions. However, she was afraid, or maybe grateful, that the particulars of last night were forever obscured.

The original sitting room between the master and mistress suites had been modified into a hedonistic bathing and dressing room. Marble, multiheaded shower, tub deep enough to dive into, and steam room were all state-of-the-art miracles, especially that fantastic steam room that had turned Caroline into a gloriously limp piece of spaghetti.

The dressing room section of the bath surrounded her with the scent of Brandon. Using his soap, wrapping his towel around her, running his brush through her hair felt intimate, almost invasive. Every nerve ending stood alert as she insinuated herself into Brandon's private life.

Six months. She would have six full months of living this close, day after day, with such intensity.

She opened his massive closet and chose a navy T-shirt, soft and well-worn, and a pair of thin grey-and-navy running shorts. Without a bra, the soft cotton rubbed against her sensitive nipples, peaking them. The running shorts bagged, but tightening the drawstring kept the waistband anchored around her.

When she checked the mirror, she found a Caroline she hadn't known existed. No flash and dash like Laurel, but certainly not the little brown sparrow she'd overheard friends and family call her. She looked tousled and sexy, like the morning after a long night of lovemaking.

But it wasn't going to happen. Theirs was a business arrangement only.

Her body ached from wanting and disappointment while a little voice deep inside asked, *Why not?*

She had always wanted her first time to be special, meaningful, a gift to carry in her heart. Was she asking too much? No. She didn't think so.

She checked her watch. She was running out of time.

Caroline didn't even give half a thought to calling for a car and driver. Having to wait on some stranger to pick her up when she was used to going when and where she pleased was not worth the luxury of a Town Car and chauffeur. She would not loose her independence along with her whole lifestyle.

With her purse on her shoulder and her dress draped across her arm, she carefully locked the door, made a mental note that she needed a key, and left the house a married woman, where she had entered single and unencumbered less than twelve hours earlier.

She just hoped no one saw her in her borrowed clothing, her hair flat from no curling iron and her face clean scrubbed from no cosmetics. But then, who did she know in this neighborhood except Ursula? And apparently, Ursula had already seen her at her drunken worst last night. Her head chose that moment to start throbbing again as a succinct reminder. Never again, she vowed. Never again.

Flashes popped to her left and to her right. People with cameras obscuring their faces emerged from behind bushes, out of trees, and even from behind her own car.

Paparazzi.

They converged on her, jostling each other at Brandon's garden gate.

Going back wasn't possible. She had heard the definite click of the door locking behind her.

With chin up, she walked toward them. They shouted questions like "Are you the other woman? Were you planning Laurel's wedding while sleeping with her groom? How long has your affair been going on under the nose of Brandon D'Estrehan's fiancée?"

What had she stepped off into? Was she Alice fallen down the rabbit hole?

For one brief, horrifying second, her brain stopped functioning, and she froze. Then one intrepid reporter called out, "Are you pregnant?"

No. No, she wasn't. She hadn't even had sex yet, right? She would feel different, look different, wouldn't she? Of course, she would.

"I am *not* pregnant," she answered him.

Nor would she be while she was under contract to Brandon. Under contract sounded so much saner than married.

She waved them off amid a plethora of "excuse me's" and "pardon me's" on her part and "Caroline, look this way" on theirs. They took plenty of close-ups while she climbed into her car. Her only hope was that the flush warming her face faintly resembled properly applied cosmetics.

Grace and dignity, Caroline. Her parents would see these photos, so she smiled happily and tried to be courteous. Mom had always told her that grace and dignity could get a woman through any situation, but then Mom had never imagined this one.

As she pulled away from the curb, a huge SUV pulled alongside her. A man hung halfway out the open window, camera pointed her direction. She swung the sun visor to block his view. The media that had surrounded Laurel was nothing compared to this mob.

Honking her horn, she bluffed her way through.

Her cell phone buzzed, distracting her as it rattled in the console. The caller ID revealed Brandon.

She almost let it go to voice mail. Instead, she had an overwhelming need to hear his voice, to assure herself that all this was real.

"Hello?"

Another car pulled in front of her and tried to crowd her to a stop.

"Where are you?" Brandon's bark grated on her frayed nerves, not at all the reassurance she'd been hoping for.

"Look, I'm busy. I'll have to call you back." She flipped the phone closed and threw it into the backseat. As she maneuvered through the Garden District's narrow lanes, the media hot on her heels, Caroline realized she was actually enjoying herself.

Who would have thought it? The quiet little sparrow actually enjoyed being in the limelight.

She arrived at her gated garage, entourage behind her. As she opened the gate and pulled in, leaving them all behind, she took a cautious breath. Surviving her first foray with the paparazzi was one thing, surviving the phone call to her parents would be another.

Once inside her apartment, she took a moment to catch her breath. As she put the kettle on for tea, chamomile and ginger to sooth her unsettled stomach, she looked around at the home she would be leaving soon. All her photos and keepsakes and everyday clutter that only yesterday had given her comfort and pride today felt like someone else's, as if she had walked into an apartment that belonged to a different person.

But then, she was a different person. Today, she was Mrs. Brandon D'Estrehan, wife to one of the richest businessmen and most eligible ex-bachelors in the world.

As she sipped her tea, she dialed her father's cell phone number. It rang and rang until finally rolling over to his voice mail. While leaving a message wasn't her bravest route, she had just about used up her store of courage for today. And before noon, too.

"Dad? It's me, Caroline. Guess what? I got married!" She forced enthusiasm into her voice. "I took a page from your book and eloped! I'll email you details later. Love you. Mom, too."

With a deflated sigh, she broke the connection. A wave of exhaustion hit her. A glance at her watch showed she had half an hour. Only half an hour to dress to meet the only man who had ever seen her naked.

Chapter Seven

Brandon checked his watch again.

She was late. Fifteen minutes and counting. Her lack of promptness hadn't been in her dossier, and for some reason he couldn't explain, he hadn't figured her as the habitually late type.

The security firm he'd hired had tailed her to her apartment since she had chosen to drive herself. The driver had called to report that she hadn't left yet but he had managed to disperse the mob that had followed her there. Brandon would need to include a talk about personal safety as well as about responsibility.

After his provoking night, he was not in the best of moods and had work to do. This meeting had not been on his schedule. But after calling and calling and then being hung up on, he was worried. Too late for second thoughts, he wanted to remind her. A deal's a deal.

The details of the banking account he'd opened for her rested in his briefcase, his part of the bargain. Now she needed to fulfill hers.

His phone rang. A quick glance at the caller ID showed

him that Mrs. Willoughby had put through his newest Asian contact.

"Hello," he said in English then switched to Mandarin and followed up with the traditional social formalities. Yes, this call was exactly what he needed. Concentrating on the intricacies of negotiation using a difficult language would keep his mind occupied while he waited for his wife.

Caroline darted and wove through traffic, catching glances at her watch as if she could slow time. Or rewind the past.

If so, would she rewind to yesterday before she demanded payment and ended up engaged and then married, or would she only rewind to last night, before she ended up in Brandon's bed sans clothing?

This trek to Brandon's office was like déjà vu. Had it only been yesterday morning she had followed this same route to his office door with intentions to demand payment for a cancelled wedding? How had she ended up marrying him?

The heavy antique ring on her finger was proof that yesterday's ceremony hadn't been an elaborate dream. How much of last night *had* been a dream?

And how did she face her new husband in the light of day?

She pulled into the parking lot and checked her watch. Twenty past noon. She was late.

Today, no throngs of sign-holding women blocked her entrance to Phoenix Rising's home offices. Instead, two men in dark suits flanked the entrance. At her approach, one of the men spoke into his cufflink while another opened the door for her. "Good afternoon, Mrs. D'Estrehan."

Caroline had the strongest urge to look behind her to see who he had spoken to. The name felt uncomfortable, like a new pair of shoes that fit too tight.

As she walked into the building, everyone she met greeted her with "Hello, Mrs. D'Estrehan," or "Welcome, Mrs. D'Estrehan," or "Congratulations, Mrs. D'Estrehan." What had Brandon done? Plastered posters of her all over the building? Had Mrs. Willoughby sent out a memo?

Yes, probably. Caroline could imagine the efficient Mrs. Willoughby emailing all Brandon's employees with Caroline's dossier photo and the news of their wedding.

Mrs. Willoughby wasn't at her post, but then, it was lunchtime. Even paragons had to eat.

Caroline paused in the entrance of Brandon's open doorway. Grace and dignity. She repeated her mantra—for all the good it had done her yesterday in this very office.

Her new husband was on the phone, his back to her, speaking fluent Mandarin. She knew nothing about this man. Nothing but what the tabloids exploited, anyway.

His shoulders stiffened, and his tone of voice suggested he was wrapping up his conversation. Shyness inundated her. Would he look at her with intimacy in his eyes? She had to lock her knees to keep from walking away.

He turned around and put down his phone. His eyes met hers then moved lower, as if he could see right thought her clothes. She had to clench her fists to keep from covering herself as she remembered Brandon's hands on her bare skin. No amount of grace could stop that memory.

That uncanny instinct he sometimes had made him look up. Her reflection was ethereal in the window glass. There she was, hurrying toward him in a soft cream summer sweater and slim off-white trousers. She was a vision of elegance.

Doing something he'd never done before, he rushed his business call, forcing it to an end when he had just gained the upper hand in his bargaining. But he had a more immediate problem to conquer.

She stood before him, her eyes unsettled. He didn't need super-vision, only memory, to know exactly what was under that prim and proper outfit.

He wanted her with a desire so strong he couldn't stand to greet her. He had lusted before. This was different. More, so much more.

His mind as well as his body shouted a primal chant of possession. Possession and protection, as if she belonged to him, belonged by his side, under his shielding arm, next to his heart.

This was ridiculous. He didn't do belonging, and he would be damned before he let a few spoken vows and a marriage contract interfere with his life. It was a contract just like the hundreds of contracts he'd executed in the past few years. A merger that benefited both parties. That was all.

And this contract had an escape clause. Six months. In six months, he and Caroline would have experienced a mutually satisfying partnership, and they would move on.

"Please, come in." He stood, holding a portfolio in front of him and gestured toward his visitor's chair. "Have a seat."

"I'm so sorry I'm late." Caroline took a step forward, breaking his stare. "I can't remember ever sleeping this late before."

Looking at her, seeing the apology in her eyes, he couldn't hold onto his annoyance. "We had a busy evening."

"Yes, we did." Caroline settled into the chair. "And a busy day as well. I'm still trying to comprehend *everything* that happened."

Not ready to address last night's sleeping arrangements, he ignored her emphasis on the word *everything*. Instead, he cleared his throat, readying himself to give Caroline distinct instructions.

From the corner of his eye, he saw Mrs. Willoughby

return from lunch. Quietly and discreetly, she closed his office door, but not before giving him a chastising frown. But winning over Mrs. Willoughby wasn't on Caroline's list of job requirements. Being his spouse was.

"We entered into a partnership. I would offer you a toast but I think we did enough of that last night." Brandon took his own seat behind his desk. She looked so prim and proper, so classy, with her hands clasped together in her lap.

Pearls. Pearls would be perfect for her.

"No. No more toasting." She rubbed her temple. "Last night I drank my quota for the whole year."

"Headache?"

"Not as bad as it was. Thank you for your thoughtfulness. The antacid—" She licked her lips. "The bed."

"You're welcome. Any time."

She gripped the chair's arms and leaned forward, looking him straight in the eye. "It won't happen again."

Could she have said anything more challenging? More inciting? "Who are you trying to convince? Me or yourself?"

How long had it been since he'd had to work to get a woman into his bed? He went over the list in his mind. So long he couldn't remember.

"As I recall, Caroline, you're the one that made things interesting last night. Wasn't that you begging me to undress you?"

"That was a mistake. I'd had a stressful day and way too much to drink. A gentleman wouldn't mention anything that would embarrass a lady."

"Ah. I see your confusion. You believe I'm a gentleman. I always hang my manners on the bedpost when I share a bed. Civility makes for such a remote bed partner. But I'll do the polite thing now and issue you an open invitation. You're welcome in my bed any time."

"That wasn't part of our bargain."

"Your negotiating point. Not mine. I'll certainly not hold it against you should you decide to take advantage of our situation."

"I'll sleep with you when New Orleans bans all bars on Bourbon Street." Which meant, of course, never.

But Brandon relished the challenge. After being hunted for so long, being the hunter made his blood run hot. Like all good hunters, he wasn't adverse to playing with his prey for his best advantage.

As if her decision didn't matter to him one way or the other, he said, "That's up to you."

A myriad of emotions crossed Caroline's face, confusion at his easy capitulation, a tinge of affront, a glimmer of disappointment at her easy victory, and relief. The relief certainly put a check on his ego. Or was it something else?

Caroline smiled, her first directed at him that he could remember. "Good. I'm glad we have that established." She settled back into her chair, as if she really believed the topic of discussion had been put to bed.

If she only knew she was being played. He would let her bluff through this first hand to sweeten the pot, but he had every intention of winning the game.

He sat back behind his desk and pushed the portfolio toward her. "You'll find a debit card and checkbook to a joint account that I've set up for you to settle your bills. I'll make regular deposits on your behalf, so feel free to use it for day-to-day incidentals and come to me if you have any large expenses that I should cover."

"Thank you. That won't be necessary." Caroline clasped her hands in her lap, looked away, then looked straight into his eyes. "I feel bought and paid for already. I don't expect you to take care of my living expenses."

"It's part of the job. As my wife, you are expected to project a certain image. That will require funds."

She hesitated, but thought better about protesting anymore. "Oh. Yes, of course. I wasn't thinking along those terms."

So this is what if feels like to be a kept woman. But she wasn't standing there with her hand out. She had agreed to work for her keep, and she intended to keep her part of the bargain.

"Since I won't share your bed, what other wifely duties would you have me perform?"

"I thought you'd never ask. What's your specialty?"

Was that a teasing glint in his eyes to go along with the hint of a grin on his lips?

Caroline was amazed. She hadn't pegged him as the teasing type. But then, she didn't really know what type he was, did she? Only what the media said.

She was quickly coming to like this personal side of her new husband.

"I'm a good cook. How about breakfast and dinner every day?"

"Maybe. Do you darn socks?" Definitely a tease.

"Does anybody? What if I promise to shop for your socks whenever you need them?" That sounded a lot more intimate than Caroline had meant it to.

"Personal chef and shopper are all very well, but can you stay awake during three-hour luncheons and awards presentations?"

"You drive a hard bargain, but I think I can manage that."

"Then you have my undying admiration." Brandon turned serious. "My public relations specialist has worked up a schedule. But I want to ask you about a particular event before she joins us."

"Sounds important."

"Yes, and potentially tricky. I'd like to have a gathering Friday after next."

Caroline's planning logic kicked in as she started making a mental checklist. "In two and a half weeks? What kind of gathering?"

"I guess you'd call it a wedding announcement party. I'd like to show you off."

"Is that a polite way of saying you want to show all your business associates that your world is stable and in control?"

"Exactly." He smiled, showing his rare dimple. "Where have you been all my life?"

"Right in your own backyard, apparently." She smiled back. Having put the sleeping-arrangement snafu behind them, Caroline felt renewed optimism that their time together might be the most interesting time of her whole life. "Give me details about this gala."

"Mrs. Willoughby has the guest list. Plan for about three hundred fifty."

"Isn't that how many were on your original wedding invitation list? This wouldn't be the same list, would it?"

Brandon had the good sense to look concerned. "I know it might make things awkward for you, but those are my business associates. I don't have another set to invite."

Caroline thought back to Paula's phone message. Every one of those guests would be seeing her as the woman who broke up Brandon's cancelled wedding.

What was that old Chinese curse? *May you live in interesting times?* But then, earning the huge amount of money Brandon would be paying her would be worth some heartache, wouldn't it?

"Where would you like to hold this party?"

"The workmen should be done with the downstairs by then. I'm hoping you will work with the decorator to get all the final touches in place."

"I can do that." Already, her mind raced with plans for the house and plans for the party. This affair could be the salvation of Weddings Divine.

"Great. Are you ready for the rest of your schedule then?"

Caroline grinned. "Bring it on."

Brandon buzzed Mrs. Willoughby. "Will you send in Maggie, please?"

Before she could take another breath, she heard the door handle rattle. Is this what he expected? All his employees at his beck and call? If he expected the same from Caroline, he would soon learn to live with disappointment. Jumping when a man said frog wasn't the way she intended to live, ever. Even for six months and a pile of money.

The PR specialist was young, bubbly, and very pregnant. She balanced a tray of sandwiches on one hand as she opened the door with the other. Her oversized tote bag was in danger of falling off her shoulder, and the camera around her neck threatened to swing into the tray with the slightest of wrong moves. Brandon sprang to assist her, setting the tray on his credenza.

"You should have had someone carry that tray for you," he said.

"I'm pregnant, not incapacitated." She winked at Caroline. "Not that I mind taking advantage of my condition. Remember, boss, that I'm in a delicate way when I give you the media report."

She offered her hand to Caroline as she introduced herself. "Maggie Sharpe."

"Caroline Duplessis. D'Estrehan." Caroline added as an afterthought. "I imagine our whirlwind wedding has kept you busy these last two days."

"Not as busy as I'm about to keep you." From her tote, Maggie handed over a leather-covered Blackberry. "I was surprised to hear that you are already willing to jump in and take on the hostess role for Phoenix Rising. The company has been needing to show a softer, kinder face for a while, and I must say, I think you'll be perfect for the job."

Maggie took the visitor's chair next to the one Brandon had just vacated. "Let's take a look at your schedule. I know Brandon said that you've planned a honeymoon for later, but still, I've built in a week of downtime before your first appointment. When I was newly married, I remember needing a period of adjustment to reorient my world."

"Thanks." Caroline couldn't help but like Maggie.

"Don't thank me yet. You haven't seen the following weeks. Plus, that will give us time to interview for your personal assistant and decorate your office."

"Office?"

Brandon looked up from his e-mail. "You might like to keep your work life separate from our home life." His sharp tone said louder than words that was his preference.

"Brandon has already designated a nice office suite for you and your personal assistant to use."

"The office sounds lovely, but I don't know that I'll need a personal assistant. I'm fairly good at organization," she said with her own Southern steel in her voice.

She would not let Brandon dictate terms to her beyond their contract, and she certainly didn't need an employee on the D'Estrahan payroll reporting her every move back to the boss.

Not that she'd have anything negative to report, but it was the principle of it all.

As she opened the calendar, she saw a liberal smattering of dates had events already entered.

Maggie leaned over to share Caroline's views. "These are all pending your approval, of course. And there are other invitations on the B list I'd like you to look through."

The weight of responsibility pressed down on Caroline's shoulders. When Brandon had explained her duties, she hadn't understood that she would actually be an integral part of his company. Why her? She was fairly certain he hadn't expected the same from Laurel.

What about her own business? Weddings Divine might not be the conglomerate that Phoenix Rising was, but it was just as important to her. And with the infusion of cash Brandon had promised her, she had a lot of repairs to make.

"Who has gone to these functions in the past? What if I have a conflict?"

As if the light moment between them had never happened, Brandon's eyes took on his characteristic unreadable flatness.

He moved to stand behind her and look over her shoulder, leaning in close, so close the fine hairs on the back of Caroline's neck stood to attention. "Why would you have a conflict?"

He dominated the space around her, as if he owned all the air between them. Caroline drew in a deep breath, taking in his scent.

She had an important stand to take, and she needed to take it now, but she had to fight hard to be coherent as her senses were bombarded by the essence of Brandon.

She swallowed. "I have my own business to run, remember?"

"Do you have any conflicts right now?" He knew well she didn't. How could she have forgotten his ruthless reputation? Nothing stood in the way of what he wanted, especially not her little failing business.

But Caroline had promised him her time, not her soul. "As Weddings Divine builds back, there will be conflicts. Do I need to remind you about why I have no clients at this moment?"

"No, *sweetheart*, you don't."

The not-so-subtle reminder of their supposed love match

did the job of silencing Caroline, but the conversation was far from over. She would postpone it until necessary, but she wouldn't avoid it.

In the silence, the tension became so thick Caroline could swear she heard it rumble like thunder.

"Excuse me." Maggie put her hand to her stomach. "I hate to interrupt this little spat, but all this confrontation is making my stomach queasy. I could use a sandwich."

Like quicksilver, Brandon pulled back all that intensity and replaced it with concern.

"You should have said something earlier." He tempered his growl as he retrieved the plate of sandwiches and fruit for Maggie and insisted she eat one immediately.

So pregnant women were truly his Achilles' heel, and he didn't even notice that Maggie was blatantly using it to her advantage. But then, it was a blind spot Caroline would never be able to take advantage of.

As Maggie munched, she gave Caroline a grin. "I think you're going to be good for him."

Caroline grinned back. "Me, too."

"He can hear you," Brandon said between bites, and the tension dissipated along with his overbearing attitude.

They finished their light meal in short order, and Brandon checked his watch. "I believe you said something about a media report, Maggie?"

"You're not going to like it."

Brandon's face took on the same grimness Caroline had watched on the wedding video. "Let's get it over with."

"I've got early copies of a few tabloids, if you want to see them. But there's really nothing you need to do. I've already issued statements to the media and threats to the gossip magazines.

Maggie shuffled a few of the newspapers, reluctantly giving them over when Brandon reached for them.

Caroline saw an old snapshot of herself in the top one and took it from Brandon. Paula had taken the opportunity to let the world know that she had always thought of Caroline as a tag along. She mentioned Caroline's secondhand prom dress and her father's teacher's salary. "She's always been like a little brown sparrow," she'd said, sharing the hated moniker with the rest of the world. Caroline handed it back.

"Problem?" Brandon asked.

"It seems I've just lost my best friend."

He pointed to the photo of Paula in the paper. "This one?"

Sadly, Caroline affirmed, "Yes." Loneliness brought tears to her eyes.

Brandon looked as if he would rush out the door immediately to avenge her honor. He exchanged glances with Maggie, and she nodded. "I'll take care of it, boss."

The cryptic statement sounded too ominous in tone for Caroline to let it pass. "Let it go, Brandon. Please. I'd rather get through this with my pride intact, and I can't do that if you rush out to fight my battles for me."

Brandon looked into her eyes, his own showing a barely controlled need for action. "Your call."

She could tell by the set of his mouth that relinquishing took all his willpower.

From teasing to intimidating to protecting in minutes. Would she ever understand this complex man? But then, she didn't have forever. She'd be willing to bet that six months wouldn't even make a dent in her study.

Maggie took the rest of the papers from Brandon, stuffed them in her tote, and pulled out copies of a press release and handed them around. "I sent this out last night as we discussed, but the celebrity TV shows had already found out about your marriage license being filed. I suspect they have a source at the courthouse, but it's too late to plug that leak."

"And?" Brandon looked like a snake about to strike.

"The bigger networks have bought footage of Caroline's car outside your residence and of the judge, Jack, and an unidentified woman entering your house to air during their celebrity features." She winced as she delivered the next part. "The judge made a rather rambling statement about performing a hasty wedding, but the woman stopped him from saying anything else."

"Then what?"

"Then there's a time lapse with Caroline's car still outside your house and Caroline coming out." She gave Caroline a sympathetic smile. "They're making a big deal about your morning-after look. The film clip will run nationally tonight."

Caroline blanched. "Are you sure?"

Maggie nodded. "I've got my own inside source. I should probably warn you that the headlines are not flattering."

Caroline's throat felt thick. "What are they saying?"

"They're referring to you as the wedding breaker instead of the wedding maker." Maggie lay a hand over Caroline's. "I'm sorry."

"Your plan for damage control." Brandon's tone was quiet and lethal.

"Emphasize Caroline's position as First Lady of Phoenix Rising. The reminder of power and wealth will dampen some of the more outrageous suppositions." Maggie held up her camera. "Leak intimate photos of the happy couple to the news and celebrity agencies that have impeccable reputations. How do you feel about interviews, Caroline?"

"I broke out in hives during my high school speech class."

"Then that's probably a no." Maggie shrugged. "I can put together press kits and distribute them with the photos."

"You're working with legal, right?" Brandon questioned.

"Of course, but that will take time. Fighting fire with fire is much quicker."

"Do it." Brandon snapped.

Maggie arranged them in various formal poses, sitting and standing, and took several shots before she stopped herself. "These aren't going to do it. I don't have the lighting for a formal portrait. Besides, I need something with more spark to capture attention. How about a kiss?"

Obligingly, Caroline stood on tiptoe to kiss Brandon on the cheek.

"Much too tame," Maggie said.

Brandon swooped in close and lifted Caroline's chin so he could look into her eyes. "How's this?"

Nervously, Caroline licked her lips. Brandon's eyes darkened and Caroline felt a great zing of heady power.

She'd always been the quiet one in her group. The reliable, dependable best friend. Never the femme fatale. But Brandon's reaction made her feel sensuous, even sexy.

Her gaze dropped to his mouth. Tentatively, she pressed her lips to his, letting herself absorb his taste, his body heat, his unique presence.

The camera clicked in the background like an annoying gnat not worth her attention.

Caroline's kiss might be enough to satisfy a doubting audience, but it wasn't nearly enough to satisfy Brandon. No doubt about it, her public kiss was igniting a fire in private places.

When she would have broken off the kiss, he wrapped his arms around her and pulled her close, letting her feel what she did to him.

Brandon let all his frustration, all his pent up energy explode as his mouth touched hers.

After the slightest of hesitations, she met him breath for breath, showing him a sensuality she wouldn't have imagined behind her reserved façade. She made it hurt so good. He knew his only relief would come from finishing what she had started with her striptease last night.

Unless, of course, she was as innocent as his sixth sense was shouting at him. He had to stop this, stop himself, before he took a step he couldn't reverse.

Caroline swayed toward him, and he put his hands on her waist to steady her. What was she doing to him? He'd never let his emotions show like this, especially in a business setting. He brushed her hair from her cheek, feeling very proud of the dreamy look in her eyes and the softness of her mouth.

And very sure she'd never been kissed like this, much less anything more.

What kind of deal had he gotten himself into?

Chapter Eight

When Brandon rubbed his thumb across her lips, Caroline thought her knees might fold under her.

Maggie brought them back to reality. "I'm convinced. I've already sent out the press releases with all the right words and phrasing about your marriage, but now I can honestly say that I've seen the evidence with my own eyes that you married for love, not money."

The blatant lie in Maggie's words brought Caroline back to her senses. Of course, it was all about business. She would not forget again, no matter what Brandon's mouth did to her.

She gave up her rigid control over her knees and sank into her chair.

Without a word, Brandon handed her a cup of hot coffee. First the antacid, now the caffeine. The man did seem to know what she needed without asking. Before she realized it, she had tightened her thighs together. Yes, after her response to his kiss, he probably knew that too.

She could feel him watching her, but didn't dare meet his eyes. Not until she got sense and sensibility under control. Instead, she gave her full attention to Maggie as she scrolled through the shots she had taken.

"Did you get what you need?" Brandon's voice was husky. Nice to know he was affected, too.

"Oh, yeah. These are great!" Maggie's eyes sparkled as she scrolled through, evaluating the shots. "These are so hot, I could probably sell them to a romance publisher for book covers. Do I have both your permissions to release these to the public?"

Brandon looked like he was making a monumental decision. "Yes. And send me a copy."

Caroline still couldn't string a sentence together, so she nodded her agreement.

"Great. I'll get these sent right out."

Maggie stood to leave, and Caroline forced herself to stand, also. She didn't need to be alone with Brandon now. She wasn't thinking clearly enough to protect herself against that famous charisma. "I'll walk out with you."

Using all her willpower, she avoided a backward glance and closed the door behind her.

She had almost made it to safety when the elevator doors refused to open. Even in her heels, she should have taken the steps, for her heart's sake.

"Caroline, wait." Brandon called, his footsteps catching up with her. "There is something further we need to discuss in private."

He put his hand on the small of her back to guide her into his office. Where his fingertips made contact, she was certain her skin must be glowing, perhaps with cartoon sparks shooting forth, too. That kiss had been cinematic.

Although she'd have to admit she'd forgotten all about Maggie and her camera until Brandon recalled her to her senses.

She wasn't worldly like him, but she was pretty certain instinct had taken over where experience left off.

Not that she shied away from men—they just rarely noticed her, especially with all her vibrant, stunning friends around.

She looked up at Brandon as he closed his office door, and her breath caught at the passion in his eyes.

Is that what the private discussion was all about? Taking that kiss beyond the view of a camera lens?

She'd never felt so much from a single kiss before. Was it Brandon's experience that made the difference?

If they shared another kiss, would they get the same results? Somewhere deep inside, she felt more than heard an uncertain maybe. And that maybe covered a lot of questions.

Instead of taking her in his arms, he indicated the visitor's chair she was fast coming to resent. He towered over her, leaned on his desk, and crossed his arms, a posture not at all conducive to kissing.

"You're a virgin aren't you?"

"What?" Was there any better way to wipe the stars from a woman's eyes? "Why do you think that?"

"That kiss."

"What was wrong with that kiss?" She stood up herself, unable to take his allegation sitting down. "It was a great kiss." She pointed at his chest then let her finger drift downward. "I could tell you thought so, too."

"Are you or aren't you a virgin?"

"It's none of your concern."

"You're my wife. Everything about you is my concern."

"That's not what the contract says."

"To hell with the—" He took a deep breath, putting on his stoic mask as he exhaled. But she knew, she'd seen behind his impassive pretense.

He smirked. "I think you've answered my question."

"You didn't need to ask it."

"I suppose not." He bent and picked up her banking

folder where she had let it fall and handed it to her. "Apologies for delaying you. I'm sure you've got plenty to do today."

She snatched it from his hand. "Yes, lots of money to spend." Turning around and walking out on him wasn't nearly as hard as it had been a few short minutes ago.

Brandon winced as Caroline slammed his door. If Mrs. Willoughby were a gossip, it would soon be over the whole building that the newlyweds had had their first fight. But she was the soul of discretion, if not full of light and joy.

Still, it was reassuring to remember that his office was completely soundproof with the door closed. At the time he'd made the renovations, he'd thought he'd been protecting the company against corporate espionage, not common gossip.

Brandon scrubbed his hand through his hair.

Caroline's virginity changed everything. He never took unfair advantage in a business deal, and he wasn't about to start now.

Taking Caroline to bed wouldn't turn business into pleasure, as he had originally hoped. It would turn business into personal, and he didn't do personal, especially with a virgin.

He had never had a desire to initiate an innocent. Too many strings attached. Too much misconstrued intensity. Too much emotional baggage to discard afterward.

Caroline apparently didn't play the game that all the other women he'd ever associated with had been playing for quite a while. Who would have guessed, when she agreed to marry him for money, that she would be so untouched by the world? Yes, he had known she was different, but he hadn't recognized what the difference was. Now he knew.

And he wanted her even more.

No matter how much he desired her, she was off-limits.

Six months. This whole business deal would be over in six months. Until then, he would abide by the terms of the contract and make their arrangement work for both of them.

He might have a reputation for being ruthless, but he also had one for being ethical.

He would do what he always did, bury himself in work, and they'd both come out better for it. At least, they'd neither be the worse for it. He'd make sure of that.

Caroline sat alone at the dining room table as the candles burned down. The grandfather clock in the hallway chimed half past nine. Staring back at her was the photo Ursula had taken during their wedding, now framed and sitting on the sideboard. The photo was her only wedding gift besides the pots and pans Brandon had ordered to be delivered this afternoon.

The card read, To my wife, to commemorate our wedding day. She figured she owed Mrs. Willoughby thanks for that.

When she'd opened them, Ursula had given her a wry smile and said, "At least it didn't come with a vacuum cleaner and a mop."

"He couldn't have picked anything better." Hope clogged Caroline's throat as she explained, "I've always wanted to explore my culinary side. I didn't think he was even listening to me when we talked about it—but he was."

"Girlfriend, never doubt that husband of yours hangs on every word you utter. Anyone who has seen you two together can tell he's fascinated by you."

No matter how hard Caroline tried to discount Ursula's erroneous observation, she couldn't help thinking about it as she cooked their first meal together.

Having her new husband show up for that meal would have made her gift complete.

Alone, she scooped up a bowlful of gumbo made from

her great-grandmother's recipe and took a bite. It was perfect. The fresh seafood blended with the vegetables she'd had handpicked from the farmer's market, and the carefully chosen spices popped. But she might as well be eating dehydrated soup without the water.

She'd like to be disappointed with Brandon, but she could only be disappointed with herself. She'd set false expectations. Brandon had never promised her anything but money.

And she had spent quite a bit of it today, clearing up all her debts and planning for their party.

The darker the night turned, the greater the house seemed to loom around her.

She tried taking a good book to bed, but her bedroom smelled of wallpaper paste and new paint, making her nose burn. Although the furnishings were lovely, they weren't hers. The room felt like a very expensive hotel room, not her bedroom. Besides, she felt too restless to settle into bed so early.

So, after cleaning the kitchen, she chose Brandon's study to leaf through her newest bridal magazines. Not that she would be needing them any time soon. As hard as she'd fought for time to take care of her business, with her full calendar, she saw none on the horizon.

Besides, Wedding Divine's phone wasn't exactly ringing twenty-four/seven. Who would to hire a groom snatcher?

As she flipped past the designer gowns and the perfect wedding cake, she couldn't help thinking back to her own cakeless wedding, the sundress she vowed she would burn at the next opportunity, and the hurricanes she promised herself she would never drink again.

And the husband she would never bed.

Then again, it was a very nice sundress. Maybe some vows were made to be broken.

Brandon saw his porch light on from two blocks away. The sight affected him more than he would have ever guessed. He'd always returned to a dark house, dark and lonely. That's why he spent most of his nights in the penthouse apartment above his office.

But tonight he kept getting an urge to come home even while he watched the clock, waiting for business hours to roll around in Kathmandu for his conference call.

Over and over, he remembered the passion in Caroline's eyes as she left his office.

The sound of that door slamming seemed to echo in his head. If he could only slam the door closed on his libido as easily as Caroline had on him.

He unlocked the door and followed the light into his office. Caroline half sat, half lay asleep on his couch, her cheek resting on her hand, a magazine on the floor. He winced when he noticed how her spine twisted. She would have a very sore back in the morning if he left her there all night.

But waking her meant damping down his desire to take their office kiss to its rightful conclusion. With any other woman, he would have pulled out all his tricks to make sure this night—make that morning—reached its fullest potential.

Except now he knew what made Caroline different. Her first time was worth more than a simple conquest for the sake of a win. He ached to touch that soft, feminine skin.

Damn, it hurt to be noble.

Caroline blinked, her eyes hazy. A soft smile turned her lips up. Then she blinked again, and her mouth took on a harsher line as she pushed herself into a sitting position.

"What time is it?"

"Early." Brandon had never, in his whole life, felt a compulsion to justify his actions. But under her wary gaze, he found himself explaining. "I had an international call to make, so I stayed late at the office and caught up on paperwork."

"You missed dinner. I made gumbo."

"You cooked for me?"

"I said I would."

"It's been twenty years since anyone cooked for me."

"Twenty years? You were still a boy."

"Yeah." He'd been twelve when he'd been wrenched from his grandparents' loving care and returned to his mother.

"Well, it may be another twenty if you don't show up or at least call and let me know you're not coming. What if you were lying in a ditch somewhere? How would I know to come looking for you?" Caroline put her hand over her mouth, stopping herself. "I'm sorry. I have no right."

He should have bristled at her dressing down, should have felt as if his freedom was being curtailed. He always thought he would feel trapped. Instead, he warmed inside, realizing that at least one person would notice if he were dead or alive at the end of the day.

He took her hand and kissed it, giving in to the need to touch her. "Your cooking for me gives you that right. I'll be home for dinner from now on or give you a call letting you know I'll be late."

"You don't have to promise me anything."

"Yes, I do. You cook for me and I'll be here. That's our deal." He realized he was rubbing his thumb across her palm and abruptly dropped her hand.

"Our deal," she echoed. "What time do you want breakfast?"

"I'd like to head for the office by seven."

"Then I'd better get to bed."

He remembered all too well what she looked like in his bed. How was he going to survive six months? "I'm going for a run."

Caroline squinted at the mantle clock. "At two in the morning?"

"I need to unwind, get rid of some tension."

She shrugged and started to stand. Brandon held his hand out to help her. Even this small gesture of lending his strength to her made his testosterone leap higher. "I'll get the locks. Don't be alarmed if you hear me come in after my run."

If only she wasn't a virgin…. He'd had no qualms before, but his past partners, all very experienced women, had known the rules. Mutual satisfaction. No morning-after regrets. No future expectations.

And they were only a phone call away.

Right now, he couldn't recall any of their faces, much less their numbers. The thought of anyone else but Caroline in his arms had him taking another lap around the block. He might rationalize that his restraint was out of respect for Caroline as his business partner, but an inner nudging told him it was something more. Impossible, of course.

Even if he did relationships, which he never would, he certainly didn't believe they could happen so quickly. Yes, he believed in lust at first sight, but that other thing. No. That was only in the movies and in books.

Brandon ran until he couldn't run another step then dropped into bed. He dreamed of amber-colored eyes and satiny skin and awoke to the smells of breakfast drifting up the stairs.

I could get used to this, he thought.

That thought held for the next two weeks as he came home to supper on his table and awoke to breakfast each morning. If he could just get some sexual release, his life would be happily ever after.

But then, fairy tales were only pretend, like this marriage.

Still, Caroline was fast making his house into his castle. Not only did she cook for him each day, she did more and more to make his house into his home. One day it was white wicker rockers on the front porch. The next day, potted red geraniums. He looked forward to seeing what new amenity welcomed him each day.

And having Caroline to talk to was priceless. They filled the time with conversation. Politics, the state of the economy, whether the new paint chip looked more like peach or pink, all the important things that made the world work.

It worried him a bit that she and that strange artsy woman, Ursula, were becoming friends. Ursula was too Bohemian for his tastes. But Caroline's otherfriends continued to trash her character for the money the tabloids shelled out. She tried to act like it didn't matter, but when her eyes filled with tears, his heart filled with revenge. Still, she wouldn't let him do what he could to stop it.

She was as witty and intelligent as she was kind and forgiving. She had a wicked sense of humor, tinged with naughtiness. Her double entendres proved that even if her body was innocent, her wit was worldly. Her eyes lit up when he teased her in kind, and she always appreciated his dry humor that most people didn't catch. She took the art of flirting to a new, sophisticated level that had him laughing even while he burned for her.

When they talked, he imagined his grandparents' conversations must have been much the same. They were married for more than fifty years before they both passed away within weeks of each other.

Evenings were spent in quiet togetherness. Neither of them were much for television. He worked at his desk while Caroline read, or he joined her on the couch with a book of his own. She made him decaf tea, which he hated. But not when Caroline set it in front of him. She brought him decaf because she worried over his late hours.

Sometimes she would rub his back, making him more

tense than he already was, but in an entirely different way. She was so sensuous in everything she did, like when she brushed his hand when she passed him the salt, or rested her fingertips on his shoulder as she straightened his tie with her other hand, or when she casually let her thigh rest against his as she sat next to him on the couch while looking at wallpaper samples.

It was so natural, so casual, she probably didn't even notice. But to a man who had learned to flinch from touch in his formative years, it meant more than it should have.

Her touches made him ache for her, but more than that, they filled an empty place that had always ached deep inside, an empty ache that had never been filled with sex.

The cooking and the tea and the touching, she didn't have to do any of it. But she went over and beyond, making his life better—more complete.

The habits he and Caroline had fallen into certainly resembled the real thing. If Brandon didn't ache so much for Caroline's body, he might forget their whole marriage was a farce. In fact, if it weren't for that big, looming, frustration that had him pounding the pavement each evening, his life would be better than he had ever imagined it could be.

If he could just shake the unease that good things like this weren't supposed to happen to men like him, his world would be perfect. But he'd always lived for the future, and enjoying the moment was a concept he couldn't seem to wrap his mind around.

Chapter Nine

On Friday, exactly fourteen days after their wedding, they had their first argument. She should have known it was coming. She'd awoken feeling antsy.

So much togetherness bred tension awareness—maybe she should call it sexual tension—that had her nerves on edge.

Her world was Brandon. His scent. His voice. His presence. The warmth of his body when he was near and the memory of him when he wasn't.

Last night, as she lay more asleep than awake, she had been sure he was there beside her, touching her the way she hazily remembered from their wedding night. When she roused herself from her dream, she'd been disconsolate to find she was wrong. Knowing only unlocked doors stood between them, she'd had the hardest time going back to sleep, and had slept restlessly until she'd given up in the early hours of dawn.

But Brandon had been up before her. He came in from his run, sweat pouring from every pore, looking so masculine she could barely catch her breath. Before he saw her, she'd seen the tension he tried to keep hidden from her in the tightness around his mouth and the shadows in his eyes and her heart had gone out to him.

So she'd made his favorite breakfast of blueberry muffins and cheese omelets hoping it would, in some small way, lighten his load.

As Brandon munched on a hot muffin, Caroline settled in to give him an overview of her coming day. She found she liked discussing her plans with him, and on more than one occasion, she'd caught her stoic husband looking at her with appreciation in his eyes. Where she had thought she would only be a token wife, she was discovering that she could really make a difference.

And so were the people of Phoenix Rising. Yesterday, when she arrived back from a Boy Scout Appreciation luncheon, she discovered a lovely plant for her office, compliments of Mrs. Willoughby, who promised to water it each Wednesday when she watered the boss's plant.

"The staff is calling you the heart of Phoenix Rising. They're right. You are." Brandon paused with butter knife in hand. "I can't find words to thank you."

A glow filled Caroline so full she was sure she must be radiating from it. "You just did."

"So everything's ready for the party tomorrow night? Anything I need to do?"

"Got it all covered." With the unlimited budget Brandon had given her, it was the kind of party she could plan in her sleep.

"How many are coming?"

"Almost everyone we've invited. More than had planned to attend your wedding." Caroline had never received so many RSVPs so promptly. They would all be watching her, speculating that she was the cause of the original scandal.

"Why the frown? I'm sure it will be perfect."

"As long as it generates new business for Weddings Divine, I'll be happy." Although Caroline had to admit, if only to herself, she'd found her work for Phoenix Rising as satisfying—maybe even more so-than Weddings Divine. But doing fulltime charity work instead of making a living for herself wouldn't be an option in another five and a half months, so she shouldn't get used to it.

She waited for him to mention her contracted duties to him, not sure how she would answer. Instead, he raised a noncommittal eyebrow. "So what's on the agenda today?"

"Baby Cuddlers." Caroline sipped from her orange juice. "They are fast becoming my favorite charity."

"I've never heard of them."

"They're not on your list for donations, but I think they should be. Baby Cuddlers are volunteers who go to hospitals and hold the newborns, giving them a nurturing touch, letting them know that they are valued. Just a half hour of rocking an infant seems to make a big difference in how well they progress.

"The neonatal unit at Charity Hospital always needs volunteers. The nurses barely have enough time to care for the infants, much less stop and give them a calm, nurturing hugging session."

"You sound like a publicity brochure." His tone wasn't complimentary.

Immediately, Caroline felt the sunny breakfast atmosphere turn as dark and cold as the Arctic during the winter solstice.

Brandon picked up his coffee cup, took a sip, and put it down. "Bitter today."

"You made it." Caroline shoved the sugar bowl in his direction.

Brandon put down his half-finished muffin. "Don't they have families to do that?" Tension laced his tone.

Caroline bit her lip, trying not to take offense. This was more than a simple conversation. "Not all babies are born into perfect families. Some of these infants' mothers are separated from their babies at birth if they have drug problems that are out of control. Then there's postpartum depression that makes it very hard for a mother to connect with her infant."

Brandon unstiffened his neck enough to nod his comprehension. "What about fathers?"

"Some of these babies don't have acknowledged fathers, but that's not always the case. Some of the parents just can't spend as much time as they like with their newborns. Yesterday, a father came in with his two toddlers to see his new son who was born six weeks too early. The baby will be in NICU for quite a while. His wife is in intensive care with blood pressure problems.

"He could only look through the glass at his new son because he didn't have anyone to care for his toddlers while he rocked his baby. So I took the toddlers to the waiting room and told them stories for half an hour so the father could bond with his new son."

The corners of Brandon's mouth tightened. "That's not typical, is it?"

"It's not unusual."

"Isn't it more typical that some parents just don't have it in them to care for these children?"

"It's true that some people don't have their lives together well enough to give their babies the love they need. Many of these babies are preemies or have special needs and are getting stronger while they are awaiting adoption."

"Unwanted babies. That's what birth control is for."

"You're being quite judgmental, aren't you?" Caroline looked hard at her husband and saw shadows in his eyes.

She wanted to probe, but didn't know where to start. Instead, she said, "I was a surprise to my parents. My dad had intended to finish graduate school first. But both my parents say I was the best surprise that ever happened to them."

"Not all parents feel that way."

Caroline had never gotten straight the chronology of when Brandon lived where, but she knew he hadn't always lived with his mother. She waded into the breech. "You weren't a planned baby?"

"No. Just a bad mistake." He crushed his uneaten muffin into crumbles. "My father met my mother during one of his rare winning streaks. She thought he was a high roller. Can't blame her there.

"She always said that she provided him with cocktails and he provided her with an unwanted pregnancy. At least she claims he's my father. I understand there's room for doubt.

"What my father believed is that my mother worked hard at getting pregnant to convince him to marry her. The truth is that she did it for the money. When she found out there was none, she was too far along to get rid of me."

Caroline wanted it to all be a misunderstanding, but deep down, she was afraid it wasn't. "How do you know this? I know children overhear things sometimes and misinterpret them, or parents say hurtful things to each other, especially when they're going through a divorce. Are you sure?"

"Yes, I'm sure. My mother told me, every day of my life that I lived with her, how I should have never been born." He picked up his cup but didn't drink. He sloshed coffee over the rim as he put it down again.

"Oh, Brandon. She was so wrong." Caroline felt heartsick. She pushed her chair back, knowing she couldn't hug away Brandon's anguish but needing to try.

"Wrong is to bring a baby into the world without a stable set of parents. There's too many ways to prevent *surprises* from happening nowadays. No excuses." He shoved his chair back, threw his napkin on the table, and stood. "Your time and my money would be better invested into pregnancy prevention programs."

Caroline thought of the premature infant that had responded to her touch for the first time as she rocked him yesterday. And to the man who now backed away as she reached out to him. She doubted he even knew he had twitched in response to her outreached fingers.

Deliberately, she put her hand on his arm to stop him. "Brandon, every baby deserves love, and I intend to give as much as I can. I'll use my own personal funds."

"Just because they deserve it, doesn't mean they'll get it. How much love, or even proper attention, will they get once they leave the hospital?" He shrugged off her hand. "I'm through talking about this."

Even though every muscle in his face was stoically under control, his eyes shouted of his pain.

As he walked toward the door, he paused and said over his shoulder, "I'll be in conference calls and meetings all day and plan to work late tonight. Don't cook for me this evening. And you only have $457.33 left in your account. How much of an advance do you think two weeks of marriage is worth?"

Very quietly, very deliberately, he pulled the door closed with a click.

Caroline hadn't realized who much she had begun to feel a part of Brandon's life until she was shut out.

Brandon ran a stop sign and charged through two red lights as he castigated himself for all he had said. What had made him say anything?

He'd carried his deep-seated anger all his life. What had made him lose control and spew his sordid history to Caroline?

The pity in her eyes had been his undoing. He didn't need her pity. He didn't need anything from anyone. He was stronger than that. He had to be. He had too many people counting on him.

He looked up at his office suite and all it represented. Families and paychecks and futures.

He wouldn't follow family tradition and let them down.

The first thing Caroline saw when she stepped into her office was an envelope with her name scribbled in Brandon's unique handwriting sitting in the middle of her pristine desk. She opened it, and Brandon's personal check fell out along with a note. She squinted to read his impatient scrawl.

> *I've called in architects to build a short-term child care facility at the hospital so parents can visit their infants. Please consult with them on this project. Use the check for rocking chairs or whatever else the Baby Cuddlers need.*
>
> *Brandon*

Caroline rushed down the hallway to thank her generous husband, only to be cautioned by Mrs. Willoughby as she pointed to the closed door. "Conference call."

"I'll thank him later, then."

Mrs. Willoughby saw the envelope Caroline clutched. "He had me set up a trust fund for your new project. You bring out the best in him."

Caroline thought of all the ways she'd been able to contribute to the world in the last two weeks through Brandon and Phoenix Rising. "He does the same for me."

Despite his plans to stay late at the office, Brandon hurried home as soon as he could, although he was still the last one to leave the office on a Friday evening. After this morning's sour leave-taking, he wanted to see her sweet face, hear her honeyed voice, and know that his world was back in order.

He caught himself driving too fast as he threaded the narrow streets.

The porch light was on, but nobody was home.

"Caroline?" No reply.

He searched his office, the bedrooms, even the bathroom, but only his footsteps broke the silence.

"Caroline!" His shout bounced off the walls.

No. Caroline wasn't here.

Finally, he looked the last place he wanted to explore. Yes. There it was.

Caroline had left a note on the dining table. In his experience, notes like this were never good.

He should have kept his darker side to himself.

His monetary apology had been given with all sincerity. Apparently, it hadn't been enough.

He unfolded the note as if it contained poison darts then had to blink twice, even with his reading glasses on, to focus on her delicate handwriting.

We've been invited across the street for a cookout. If you get home in time, hope to see you there. Caroline

He read it again as his pulse returned to normal, glad no one had been around to see his knee-jerk reaction.

This was nothing like that other note, the one his mother had left that said he'd received birthday money from his grandparents and she would be back soon with cake and presents. Six days later, the landlord had come to collect the overdue rent, found him alone, and put him to work begging on the street corners until the local police picked him up and his grandparents came for him. It sounded like a piece of fiction straight out of a Dickens novel, but it was real enough. He had the memories to prove it.

Still, that was a long time ago. He was a grown man now. Time to get over correlating notes with abandonment. Besides, in less than six months, he would be alone again by choice. Unless... But why would she want to stay?

He glared at the house across the street, not in a partying

kind of mood, but neither did he want to stay home alone while his innocent wife laughed and flirted less than two hundred yards away.

Every time she saw him, Caroline's breath caught. She had expected to get used to his good looks after two weeks of constant contact, but she still got a jolt whenever he walked into the room. It was the same reaction she'd experienced the first day she'd walked into his office. It was worse, so much worse, than the movie-star crushes she'd had when she was thirteen. This was real.

Brandon had changed into shorts and a T-shirt, a classic male-at-leisure look that fit him just as well as his designer suits and preppy business-casual clothing. Was there anything the man couldn't pull off?

The tightness around his mouth and exhaustion in his eyes worried Caroline. He'd been putting in hours and hours on an international merger that was teetering on the brink of disaster, and he was overdoing it on the midnight exercise. Obviously running for tension relief wasn't working for him.

He waved in Ursula and Jack's general direction, but headed straight for her.

As natural as if they'd been doing it for years, he crossed over to the swing and gave her a kiss. She'd expected a chaste peck on the cheek like her parents were apt to give in public, but he pulled her from the swing and wrapped her in his arms as if he would never let her go.

His mouth sought hers, showing her a passion she hadn't tasted since that day in his office when Maggie took their photos. She willingly gave back, indulging in the desire that had been growing stronger every day.

Surely this kiss wasn't just for Ursula's sake to convince her of their pseudorelationship. His arms around her felt too real, too sincere, too needing, not just a perfunctory embrace.

Unless, of course, she was reading more into the tight clinch than was really there.

Remembering that they were just pretending was getting harder and harder while falling in love was getting easier and easier.

If anyone had told her that love could happen this quickly, she'd have disagreed. She'd have told them they were only infatuated. Now she knew better. Infatuation felt too small for what she felt.

But where did one-sided love end up?

"No more notes on tables," he whispered in her ear. "I don't like them."

So much for sweet nothings. She'd hoped for something a bit more romantic after a kiss like that. But maybe this had something to do with his revelations this morning.

His humanity was seeping through that hard exterior he showed the world. And maybe, just maybe he was beginning to trust her as a friend.

Was it too much to hope for? Friends today, lovers tomorrow, and marriage forever was her fairy-tale wish.

But she had no stars to wish upon with the overcast sky and approaching tropical storm. Thunder rumbled in the distance.

"No more notes on tables," she promised and felt the tension lessen in his shoulders before he let her go. "Thank you for the donation."

"You're welcome." He pushed away, but not before Caroline felt tension infiltrate his touch.

Jack flipped the steaks on the grill. "We've been waiting for you."

"I noticed you left early today." Brandon took a long swallow and inconspicuously flexed his shoulders. Caroline could tell he was trying to shrug off his long day. When had she begun to read the subtle signs he tried to keep hidden from the world?

"After my sixty-hour workweek, I figured I was due a nine-hour day today." Jack grinned at Ursula. "And don't expect me in this weekend, either. I've got better things to do."

"Just don't make a habit of it."

Jack handed Brandon a beer. "You should leave that boss attitude at work."

Testosterone made the air so heavy Caroline could hardly breathe. All-girls' schools and her lack of brothers may have deprived her of an education about masculine moods, but she could read this mood well enough.

When Brandon took the beer, Caroline let out her breath.

He twisted off the top. "Thanks. For the beer and the reminder. And the invitation to supper."

"You're welcome."

An awkward moment hung while the two unemotional men tried to figure out what to do with their feelings.

Ursula smoothed it over by holding up her beer in salute. "To weekends."

Jack returned the salute then turned his attention to the steaks starting to sizzle on the grill. Ursula brushed them with marinade, threatening to paint Jack with the sauce-laden brush if he burned hers.

Hadn't they only met two weeks ago? They looked so comfortable with each other for such a short time.

What did people think of her and Brandon?

The way Brandon glared at Ursula made it clear he didn't approve of their newfound relationship.

Fleetingly, Brandon narrowed his eyes as the two of them shared an intimate look.

Catching her watching him, he rubbed his hand across his face, completely wiping away any expression. But he couldn't wipe away the dark circles under his eyes.

Caroline knew he was exhausted. But if she hadn't known about his late hours, she would have never guessed how anguished he was over the negotiations. He hid his heart from the world, letting everyone only see his ruthless side. But she wasn't everyone. She was his wife. Caroline had made multitudes of cups of decaffeinated tea for both of them as she sat and read in his home office while he poured over contracts. He'd already gotten the money part worked out. He was trying to save jobs, jobs that would take away from his own personal profit but would keep men and women working.

She didn't understand all the details. She only knew that it seemed to sooth Brandon to talk to her about it, so she was there for him, listening and making sympathetic noises even as her eyelids drooped and she stifled her yawns.

As Ursula shook her beer and aimed the spray at Jack over some bantering remark, he retaliated by catching her around the waist and kissing her long and hard.

Caroline sat on the back porch swing, wistfully watching their antics wishing she could make Brandon laugh like that.

As the sun faded, the outside twinkle lights came on creating an oasis of soft light chipped from the dark. Comfortable after their meal, the four of them gathered on the porch as the fan lazily stirred the humidity-laden air. Caroline claimed the swing again, and Brandon joined her, taking the opportunity to wrap his arm around her shoulders.

Being this near to her, touching her, however so innocuously, felt more fulfilling than a major corporate conquest.

Brandon studied his wife sipping her Diet Coke. She needed a diet drink like he needed a computer virus. She was perfect, except for that melancholy look in her eyes. He wanted to put a smile on her face, to make her laugh, to make her happy.

He took full blame for the way her friends had turned on her, even her best friend from childhood. Every day her name was trashed in the tabloids from stories leaked by her ex-best friends. He couldn't imagine how painful the betrayal must feel.

He wanted to fix it, just a discreet word of warning from one of his people would do the trick, but he'd promised Caroline he'd leave it alone. Honoring her request put a knife in his gut every time he saw that sad look in her eyes. She was too good of a woman to have to suffer for this scheme of his. Even in her pain, she took care of her friends.

Before he realized what he did, he put his hand over hers, a habit he was picking up from her.

He was getting comfortable with her touching, actually looking forward to times like this when she patted his thigh as he sat next to her.

This time, she left off watching Ursula and Jack play and gave him her full attention. The most beautiful of smiles blossomed on her face as she laced her fingers through his.

Brandon had never felt more at peace. He would give anything to capture this moment in time and hold it forever. That word *relationship* floated across his thoughts. Maybe it wasn't such a bad word after all.

He had to remind himself that the clock was ticking. Less than six months—unless he could convince her to stay. Only, his track record wasn't that great in getting women to stick around. And he wasn't sure how much longer he could keep his libido in check.

As he'd diplomatically rebuffed a female CEO at one of his meetings today, he knew it wasn't a problem of finding another woman to soothe him. It was a problem of not wanting any woman other than Caroline.

Ursula snagged another beer and held it aloft in

challenge. "Let's play truth or drink."

"I thought that was truth or dare." Jack countered.

"No. This is the grown-up version. You either tell the truth or take a drink." She distributed fresh bottles all around. "But just to keep us from going overboard, here's a rule. You can only pass and drink for one out of every four questions. Deal?"

"Sounds like fun." Caroline accepted her fresh Diet Coke and sat forward, ready to reveal all.

No. No deal, Brandon wanted to say.

Caroline must have picked up on his aversion because she looked over at him with concern in her eyes. "If you don't want to…"

He refused to be the one to put a pall over the party, not with Caroline's eyes shining so bright at the prospect of this silly game. Most especially, he didn't want to see her pity again like he had after this morning's revelations.

"Fine." He hoped he didn't sound as churlish as he felt.

Caroline started with simple questions, like favorite colors—Who would have guessed Caroline's was red?—and their favorite food—cotton candy for her, boiled crawfish for him.

Then Ursula started to ask the hard-hitters. Who were their first loves, complete with breakup details. Jack and Ursula confessed to grade school crushes.

"Natalie." Brandon tossed out the name of his college live-in. She left him when he spent more time studying and working than with her.

"She came to her senses" was all the explanation he intended to give.

When Caroline's turn came, he found an illogical jealousy coloring his mood as he waited for her answer.

"Pass," she said. Did that mean she'd never had a first love? Hope lifted his mood while practicality asked why it mattered? He would never have that honor—or that responsibility. Although with her teasing and flirting, he'd been forgetting that too often.

Obviously, if she really was a virgin as he suspected, or even very inexperienced, she had her reasons for her chastity.

She would want commitment, entanglement, happily ever after.

He could never be anyone's Prince Charming, not with all his curses. He put the mood back where it should be, harmless fun. "Too many to remember, huh?"

"I don't kiss and tell." She winked at him. "My turn for a question. Where were you born?"

"Wait." Ursula stopped him from answering and pointed to Caroline. "You've got to take a drink. That's the rules."

When Caroline reached forward to retrieve her Diet Coke, her shirt gaped open ever so slightly, giving Brandon a peekaboo look. Was that a red bra she was wearing? His favorite color could become red very easily.

She held her drink high and proclaimed, "Victory to winners and losers alike" then took a deep swig.

Her toast was a timely reminder that this was just a game. Just like their whole marriage was only a game, a game he had devised himself. A game that would definitely leave him the loser in the end.

"Okay, Brandon, answer the question," Ursula instructed.

"Las Vegas," he answered.

Jack gave him a puzzled look. "I didn't know that. I thought you were a native of New Orleans like me."

Brandon shrugged away the question. "You know I've got gambling in my blood. Back then, my father thought the best action was in Vegas."

"Caroline, your turn," he said to draw attention away from himself.

She obliged by answering. "Oahu."

He already knew from Caroline's dossier that she had been born in Hawaii while her father was in graduate school.

He leaned close and pitched his voice low. "An island girl, huh? Can you hula?"

She batted her lashes. "For the right man, I can do anything."

Caroline's flirting had him wanting to grab her right then and there, toss her over his shoulder, and take her to his cave. He wanted to be wanted so badly it hurt all the way through him.

While he was still arguing himself out of the idea, Caroline thrust a beer into his empty hands and said, a touch too brightly, "Ursula's turn."

Apparently she'd used up her store of bravado. Did she want him or not? She refused to look at him even as he traced patterns up her arm. But she didn't pull away.

When Ursula hesitated, Jack urged, "How about you, Ursula?"

Ursula lifted her beer, swallowed, and said, "Pass." At Jack's raised eyebrows, she answered, "A girl gets thirsty sometimes."

As if she was daring him, she pointed to Jack. "It's your turn to ask a question." Obviously, Ursula and Jack were playing their own little side game.

Jack stared into Ursula's eyes without blinking while a pulse pounded in his neck. If they were playing blackjack, Brandon knew that Jack would be doubling down right now, going for broke. Jack was a risk taker with life as well as with cards, but then, Jack had never left the table with nothing but his name to call his own.

"First memory," Jack challenged.

Ursula looked like she wanted to refuse. Then she met him, stare for stare.

"Looking into my mother's eyes." By the lift of her chin, she dared him to ask for details.

Brandon had sat across from Jack for enough card games to know that Jack rarely knew when to throw in his hand. He'd gambled away a small fortune due to his stubbornness to lose a hand, not accepting that some nights fate was unkind, and the cards just didn't fall right.

When it came time to walk away from Caroline, could Brandon do it? Or would he lose his self-respect by trying to hang on to a predestined losing hand?

This time, Jack shrugged and said, "Good enough," letting Ursula's answer stand.

Brandon studied his friend. It seemed that Jack could change for a woman. Though by the strain around his eyes, he wasn't at ease with it.

Ursula made Brandon uneasy, too, but in an entirely different way. She had too much mystery about her for Brandon's comfort. He made a mental note to have her investigated, for Caroline's safety as well as for Jack's sake.

Ursula turned the question back to Jack. "What about your earliest memory?"

He pointed to a magnolia tree whose branches draped against the lawn. "I was right there under that tree when I found my first Easter egg."

Caroline's earliest memory was equally as innocent. She remembered being in her high chair and spewing out carrots. "I still don't like them. Brandon? You?"

Brandon's first memory was of his parents fighting and him hiding under the bed. He must have been five or so. Not a happy memory, and not one he wanted to share over a drinking game.

"I like carrots, myself."

"That wasn't the question."

"Then pass," he said and swallowed a healthy swig of

beer.

Caroline looked like she wanted to probe, but she didn't. Instead, she threw out her next question. "What was your first job?"

"You first."

"Cookie taster the time my mother started a bakery."

"You actually got paid for eating cookies? That's got to be the best job in the world," Ursula said, and they all agreed.

"It's what made me so sweet." She wiggled her fingers in front of Brandon's mouth. "Want to taste?"

Yes, he did. But he didn't want to stop at her fingertips. "I don't snack, and I always finish what I start."

She jerked her hand back. "And I shouldn't bite off more than I can chew."

He was so focused on watching the emotions change in her eyes that he didn't realize he was staring until Ursula pulled Caroline's hand over, palm up.

"My first job was telling fortunes. Shall I tell you about your future, milady?"

"Sure."

Ursula crinkled her brow, looking very serious. Then she folded Caroline's hand closed and put her hand around it as if she could lock in Caroline's future. "I see a dark, handsome, and very rich man sweeping you off your feet."

"Too late. That's my present, not my future." Caroline laughed. "What was your first job, Brandon?"

"Odds and ends, like car washing," he answered, and it was true enough. He'd rushed at cars whenever they stopped at red lights, dragging dirty clothes over their windshields until the drivers paid him to go away.

"Although I'd rather have been a cookie taster. Then I'd be as sweet as you." He distracted Caroline's intense interest by nibbling on her neck and was gratified when she didn't pull away. Instead, she rewarded him with a sultry laugh.

But the lightness didn't last. Jack and Ursula were playing their own game at his and Caroline's expense.

When Caroline asked, "What's Jack's future?" Ursula shrugged. "That's up to him. What *is* in your future, Jack?"

"I believe the question was about first jobs." He took a swallow.

"Does that mean you pass?"

"No. I don't pass just because I'm thirsty. Coward's way out." He stared hard at Ursula before answering in general. "My first job was working for Brandon, although I'd done plenty of volunteer work as a member of my Mardi Gras krewe and my fraternity."

Ursula frowned. "That doesn't sound like you, Brandon, to take on an untried person in such a key position."

"Instinct. I've hired my best people on instinct. And he worked cheap. If we didn't get the deal, neither of us made a penny. To tell you the truth, I could hardly believe he'd agree to represent Phoenix Rising under those conditions."

"At the time, I'd have done anything to keep from having to work for my grandfather. Even work for free," Jack revealed.

Ursula worried with her bottom lip before coming to some internal conclusion. "Now that makes sense."

Jack smirked. "I thought it would to a fortune teller."

"Better a fortune teller than a doomsday crier."

The undercurrents were so thick a person could drown in them.

"What's your biggest regret?" Jack challenged Ursula.

She looked deep into his eyes and said, "Not leaving soon enough to avoid this question." With that, she gave them all a wave and scurried across the yard to disappear through the hedges that separated her place from his.

Brandon took the cue and stood, grateful this game was over. After a round of good-byes which included him jealously clenching his fists while Jack gave Caroline the briefest of social kisses, Brandon led her across the street.

She stopped him on their veranda. "What *is* your biggest regret?"

He wanted to tell her the game was over. No more questions and answers. Instead, he found himself revealing, "I didn't say thank you to my grandparents before they died." He pushed a strand of hair from her cheek. "And yours?"

"Letting my parents put up their house for my business," she said without hesitation.

Which was her only motivation for marrying him, of course. He should be grateful for the reminder of reality.

She turned to go inside. "Are you coming to bed?" The way her hand dragged along his shirtfront led him to believe that he could easily turn her words into an invitation with the right response and a little encouragement.

So why didn't he take advantage of the situation, advantage of her, and give them both a night they would never forget?

Because with Caroline, it would mean more than a night. She deserved more.

He wasn't good with personal relationships. Ask any of his ex-girlfriends.

"I think I'll go for my run."

Brandon ran until his legs quivered, his reasoning pounding against his desire as his feet pounded the sidewalk. He'd always known what he wanted and hadn't hesitated to go after it.

Keeping everything impersonal had always worked for him, had kept everything under control, had kept him fed and clothed and given him a place to sleep at night.

Keeping everything impersonal had built the world he now lived in.

Emotions got in the way of assessing risk. Taking risks

was what his game had always rolled on.

Even while he'd worked his way through college, he'd learned to take risks—when he had nothing to lose, it had been his only option—and had turned around his first business, a small grocery store. He'd saved the jobs of four employees by keeping that store open. Then another business and another until he'd ended up where he was today. An exhausted, aching man sitting on stairs, looking up into the heavens and asking why.

Why was he sitting here when there was a beautiful woman upstairs who, with a little persuasion, would succumb and join him in his bed?

For the first time in his life, he hesitated to go after what he wanted, afraid he might lose what he already had.

Chapter Ten

For the twentieth time in so many minutes, Caroline unraveled the tiny hat she was crocheting while she waited for Brandon to come home. She sat in her favorite corner of his couch in the study, a room that was fast becoming as much her place as his.

The look in his eyes as he had turned from her had stopped her in her tracks. She wanted—no, she needed to tell him that her regrets were for putting her parents' lifestyles in danger, not for marrying him. Marriage to him was the best thing that had ever happened to her.

What would he say if she confessed she'd fallen in love with him?

Was this the right time? Would he believe her?

Brandon was a man of action more than words. What if she showed him?

Before she shredded the yarn, Caroline switched to a less complex baby blanket. She was on her sixth row when she heard the front door open.

Brandon came into the room limping and soaked in sweat. How did the manmade perspiration look sexy?

He raked his wet hair off his forehead. "I saw the light on. What's wrong?"

"Nothing with me. I was waiting up for you." She put down her yarn. "Did you hurt yourself?"

He shrugged it off. "I just pulled my hamstring. It will be fine by morning."

"Let me get some ice for it."

"It will be fine," he repeated.

"Obstinate man." She grinned at him to take the edge off. "Ice is no trouble. You don't want to be limping at our party tomorrow."

"Why were you waiting for me?" Brandon studied her as if he was trying to look into her soul.

Caroline willed herself to meet that intense probing without pulling back. "We need to talk."

He reacted as all typical males react to that proclamation. The shadow of doom crossed his face. "Can it wait? I'm dripping on the carpet."

"Go shower. I'll bring the ice pack up." She didn't wait for his agreement but walked past him, half expecting him to refuse out of stubbornness.

Instead, she heard footsteps behind her and then an uneven gait as he climbed the stairs.

Caroline took her time putting together an ice pack, giving Brandon time to shower. She knocked outside his door. and it swung open on its own.

Brandon whipped around, in the midst of shaking out a T-shirt. He wore only clean running shorts, just the slightest, thinnest bit of fabric keeping him modest.

Caroline couldn't take her eyes off that broad chest, those rippled abs, and the single water drop that slowly traced it's way down the line of his stomach.

As much as she would like to do otherwise, she ignored his obvious visible response as his body proved he wasn't immune to her inspection. She had to clear the air first, let him know how she felt, or it would be only sex. And she wanted it to be so much more.

She pointed to the bed. "On your stomach."

Amazingly, without hesitation or argument, he lay as instructed, crossing his arms to support his head.

The sight of this large virile male doing her bidding made Caroline's stomach quiver with need. Her hands ached to touch him, to run her palms down the length of him, to feel his warmth, his energy.

Caroline gave in to her desire under the guise of offering to massage the back of this thigh. "Before we apply ice, let me see if I can unknot those muscles a bit."

She was rather proud of herself for getting the words out without stuttering, although her voice sounded sultry and a bit breathless.

"Fine," came his muffled assent. She couldn't read anything into his single word answer no matter how hard she tried.

She rested her palm on the back of his thigh. His skin was as warm and electric as she had imagined. At her initial touch, his whole body went taut.

"Take a deep breath," she murmured.

Instead, he asked, "What did you want to talk about?"

"I think you may have misinterpreted what I said earlier about my biggest regret. I *do* regret that I risked my parents' house and almost lost it. I *don't* regret that you offered me a way out and I took it. For that I'm very grateful."

Brandon lay perfectly still, barely breathing. Caroline wanted to see his expression, but he had cradled his face in his crossed arms.

Just as she had given up on a reaction, he said, "Even if marriage to me has cost you your friends."

"They weren't very good friends if I lost them so easily,

were they? Besides, I've made new friends. I really like Ursula and Jack." She intentionally lightened the moment. "And you're not so bad, yourself."

He lifted his head and craned around to look at her. "You, either."

Caroline evaluated his understated response and chose to believe it was heartfelt.

Gently, she began to knead his hamstrings , patiently increasing pressure as his muscles responded. After a few moments, she ventured a question she had been trying to puzzle out.

"Brandon?"

"Hmm?"

"I've never put together when you lived with your grandparents. How old were you?"

Under her hands, he tensed, then blew out a breath and deliberately relaxed.

"I was eight."

"Was that when your parents divorced?"

"No, they did that when I was five."

"How did it happen?"

"The divorce? Typical story, or as typical as a story can be in my family. My grandfather turned over this house and a small fortune to my father when I was born, wanting him to come home. Instead, my dad lost it all on the roulette table. It took him all of three hours, I've been told.

"So my mother went back to waitressing, and my father found work in a small assembly plant. I can't remember that we were deliriously happy, but we were stable. Then the plant closed and Dad was laid off.

"He became a bartender and ended up with another cocktail waitress. They settled somewhere around Reno."

"How often do you talk?"

"I haven't heard from him since my grandfather's

funeral. He left as soon as the will was read and he discovered there was nothing in it for him." Brandon's back muscles visibly tightened. "I hear from my two half brothers on occasion, though. The first time I was featured in a magazine, they contacted me. I'm sending them to college. Maybe someday I'll meet them in person."

As she sorted the chronology in her mind, Caroline massaged between his shoulder blades, trying to soothe the muscles that had become as unyielding as armor.

"Why did you move in with your grandparents?"

"Someone alerted Social Services that I had never been enrolled in school. That, along with a list of other infractions, led them to declare my mother unfit. They called my father, but he wouldn't take me in. Instead, he directed them to my grandparents.

"Granmere' spent the summer teaching me to read so I wouldn't be behind the other children when school started. And Granpere' taught me how to add and subtract by teaching me how to play blackjack."

"That's an unconventional way to tutor."

"I was an unconventional kid, on the rebellious side."

"I can see that."

"Granmere' had to bribe me with pralines to get me to read."

"And your granpere'?"

"He was a wily one. He would invite over his buddies and let me play cards with them. I didn't figure out until years later what he was doing.

"We would all play cards for hours while they told stories of their lives. Their stories told me that life could be a different way than the one I had lived. They taught me to read people as well as cards, and their stories showed me a life that could be different than the one I'd been living. Those old men taught me hope."

"Why did you ever go back to your mother, then?" Shoulder muscle bunched under her probing. Gently, she worked through the knots.

"I didn't have any choice. She showed up on my grandparents' doorstep four years later with a reversal of the state's decision and demanded me back. Of course, that demand came with court-ordered child support which she knew my grandparents would pay on behalf of my father since they didn't want me to starve."

"You were twelve by then?"

"Yeah."

"Didn't your grandparents try to stop them?"

"Legally, they could do nothing. Fighting for me through the courts broke their hearts. The legal fees and the paternity support depleted what was left of their savings."

"When did they die?" Caroline caressed the muscles near the base of his head, trying to ease the strain.

"The summer I turned sixteen. I stayed in school, to honor my grandparents, but also worked as much as I could. Construction work, backroom poker games, whatever it took to keep the landlord happy and food on the table for whenever my mother came home to eat."

"Where's your mother now?"

"Dead. Overdose. She died that same summer."

"Where did you live after that?"

"I'd already been living independently, so nothing changed there. Officially, I became a ward of my father, and the authorities expected me to move in with his family, but he never mentioned it so neither did I. Mostly, I stayed out of trouble and didn't attract attention, so nobody bothered me. When I finished high school, I received enough scholarships to go to college, and you know the rest."

Caroline leaned over and placed the slightest flutter of a kiss on the back of his neck. Every touch, every breath she took soothed and excited. Brandon knew he could roll over, take her in his arms and have her. Every fiber of his body urged him to do exactly that.

But sympathy sex didn't fit his profile. He also knew he could show her things that would make her forget all about his life's story. But he didn't want this to be a one-time conquest that would be damned awkward in the morning.

He wanted—what? A commitment? But that meant an even give and take from both of them.

That meant letting Caroline in his head *and into his heart.* He'd always been on his own. He wasn't sure if he was made for a partnership of the heart, even if he wanted one. Tonight, he'd let her into his past, much deeper than any other woman he'd ever known. How much further was he willing to let her go?

How long was commitment? Forever?

Forever was a long time.

He faked a yawn. "It's late. With the party tomorrow, I've go to go into the office early and get some work done first." If she made a move to stay, he knew he would be at the end of his restraint.

"Don't you ever take a day off?"

"Why should I do that?"

"So you can play with me."

"You make the playdate and I'll schedule it. But not tomorrow. I've got problems that won't fix themselves."

Totally against his instincts, Brandon willed himself to stay still as Caroline left his bed.

"Good night, then," she whispered. "Sweet dreams."

And his dreams were sweet, full of the scents and sensations of Caroline.

But soured by frustration and the agony of not knowing what to do next.

After their late night, Caroline overslept her alarm. Brandon had already left by the time she made her way downstairs to open the door to the remodelers.

The chaos and confusion Caroline had lived for the past two weeks would soon be over. For a fortnight, work crews had tripped over decorators who then came and complained to her. RSVPs had come in from all over the world via post and e-mail and one even came in through the U.S. Embassy. Keeping account of who accepted and declined, of what paint chip went in which room, and of where she wanted the electric sockets installed was enough to make her head spin.

Yes, she needed a personal assistant, if only she had time to interview for one. With the party tonight, that was a task that would have to wait.

Her only respite had been last night's impromptu cookout. While playing Ursula's game, she had felt the rush of flirting, of being desirable and desired when Brandon teased and flirted back. And had felt the thrill of his touch, beyond charisma, beyond that initial, electrifying attraction, and deep, deep within her soul.

She'd also learned more about her husband. She was learning to read him, to see the subtle signs behind that stoic exterior. When he tried to show the world the least, he was showing her the most.

Then he had trusted her enough to willingly reveal to her a part that he kept hidden from the world. She treasured their talk, although her heart ached for the boy he had been. She'd caught the pain in his voice when he talked of his mother and father and the deep sadness of loss when he told her about his grandparents.

And she was determined that tonight she would do everything in her power to make sure that he would benefit from the man he had become.

By the time the decorator arrived for the final touches, Caroline had already answered the door to the chef and his staff and the florist.

With decorator in tow, she made a dusty trek to one of the attics and opened a huge old armoire. Four three-quarter-size oil paintings in gold-leaf frames rested inside, covered in canvas. Together, they lifted out the heavy portraits.

"These will go in the Grande Hall, don't you think?" Caroline could imagine the impressive paintings gracing the walls with their sense of heritage.

"These are perfect," the decorator concurred, "and in great condition. Your husband looks exactly like this one."

Caroline studied the cocky, debonair man in the photo. "He must have been a real heartbreaker."

The decorator grinned. "I would have let him break my heart." She rubbed a finger along the grimy frame. "I'll have these cleaned and hung by midafternoon."

A wave of jealousy shook her. They were portraits, for goodness' sake. Could she get any more unreasonable?

With a forced smile, she said, "I'll be sure to tell the florist so she can take these into consideration when she places the arrangements."

When Ursula dropped in to sample the party trays and inspect the newest changes, she raved about the portraits.

"Look at their faces. They look content, as if they've been waiting to come home," she said in her whimsical way.

Even in the most tense of times, she made Caroline laugh.

And Caroline needed a good de-stressor when she learned her parents' plane would be late. She had hoped to have a nice long chat with them before the party. Then again, maybe it was better this way. Her and Brandon's arrangement might not stand up under their prolonged scrutiny.

She stood on the veranda and watched dark clouds swirl

overhead, harbingers of the storm in the Gulf of Mexico that was making its way toward them. The weather fit her mood exactly.

The strong breeze whipped her hair into her eyes and mouth. The weatherman had assured New Orleans that this tropical storm would not develop into a hurricane, but it still had to be planned around. Several guests, including her parents, would be changing schedules to fly in before the storm moved onto land.

But the impending storm wasn't the cause of her mood, nor was facing the crowd that was sure to whisper behind their hands as they compared her to Laurel. Not even the prospect of introducing Brandon to her parents as her husband had her out of sorts—much.

It was the man she lived with that had her tied into knots.

She had cooked for him, decorated his home, even bought him new running socks as he was wearing them out at an alarming rate, and still he made no move to be any closer to her than a roommate, albeit, a very attentive one.

When her sniffles had turned into a slight fever a few days ago, he had insisted on calling her doctor himself then plied her with hot tea and antibiotics each night before bed.

Such a big fuss for a little respiratory infection. She didn't dare tell him that the doctor suspected dust and mold from the house's attic for fear he'd make her promise to stay out of it. And she was having too much fun exploring and finding heirlooms to add to the décor.

Decorating, cooking, and even planning this big party had been great fun.

If only she was having as much fun with her other wifely duty, the one that didn't involve cooking and shopping for socks. The one she had adamantly said she would never do.

Yes, she had pulled back and sent mixed signals. Okay,

maybe even no signals. But he was supposed to be the expert in seduction, wasn't he?

Did he find her unattractive? Although Caroline didn't have a lot of experience, she wasn't so innocent that she didn't recognize the physical signs of his arousal or understand his midnight runs.

Still, he'd been nothing but a gentleman. Where she thought that Jack's dinner party had them both sizzling, Brandon had cooled off to lukewarm. She should be grateful. She *was* grateful.

No. She wasn't grateful at all. She was disappointed and baffled and, most of all, frustrated. With herself as well as with Brandon.

Hadn't she been the one to set the ground rules? Hadn't she been the one to draw the line in the sand about what she would and wouldn't do?

So wasn't it up to her to change the rules? That's where she ran into trouble.

She had never vamped a man before, but she had a plan. She had given up bridal magazines for *Cosmo* and *Elle* and found them to be great resources.

Tonight would be different. She would pull out all the stops. Her dress was killer, and her attitude would be even more so.

The quiz in *Cosmo* had pinpointed her style as more Audrey Hepburn than Marilyn Monroe. She might not be flash and dash like Marilyn and Laurel, but she fully intended to end up with the guy by the end of the night, just like in the movies. Audrey always ended up with her hero in the end, too. Caroline took a long look in the mirror. Yes, she could be Audrey.

Caroline glanced at the clock. Time for a nice long soak in the tub and a nap before the party, which was exactly the advice she recommended to all her brides. Now she understood their amazement that she would even think they could sleep before their big events.

Still, she needed to try. She'd kept a tired edge about her with as little sleep as she had been getting, keeping up with Brandon's hours, then lying awake at night, knowing he was just an easily opened door away.

Although she had taken up crochet to relax, it hadn't helped much. She would soon have enough baby blankets to donate to the local Baby Cuddlers group for every infant born in the city this year.

Knowing she would forget later, she took her antibiotic and antihistamine. She lit votive candles along the tub's ledge turning the bathing alcove into a calm, meditative room all to herself. Reaching for the inner Zen Ursula was always talking about, she breathed deeply in and out. Between the medication, the hot bath, and the flickering of the candle flame, she drowsed into sleep.

The sound of the shower roused her. The thought of Brandon naked *aroused* her, wiping away all signs of sleep. It took all her will power to lie perfectly still and quiet so that she wouldn't alert Brandon that she was only a louvered door away. Then again, maybe she should splash a bit.

There were those mixed feelings again.

As soon as she heard the door to Brandon's bedroom close, she wrapped a towel around herself and called out, "Brandon?" just to make sure.

No answer. Not even a rustle of movement.

She was safe—unfortunately.

If her seduction plan was to be successful, she would have to develop a bolder attitude. Taking special care with her makeup, Caroline understood why historical tribes had resorted to war paint to hide behind. She didn't realize how much time she was taking until Brandon knocked on the door.

"Our guests are arriving."

"Ack! Be right there." Grabbing her silver lamé gown from the padded hanger, she noticed the seamstress had been a bit careless when taking up the side seams. The material bunched slightly, but the drape of the fabric should hide the slight imperfection.

Once again, Caroline ran into one of her own bride's rules, always do a dress rehearsal before the big day. But the dress hadn't been ready for pickup until yesterday, and today had been too busy. When this party was over, she would have a lot more empathy for her brides.

She stepped into the dress and tried to pull it up over her hips. Worry started worming into her heart. Too snug.

She hated to mess up her hair, but she squirmed out of the dress and tried to pull it over her head. The waist got stuck around her shoulders.

Worry exploded into panic as she wrestled it off.

She held it up and examined it. The waist had been taken in too much. Not even a child could fit into this dress. Yes, she had other gowns, but they were all at her apartment.

She had hesitated moving her things, wanting to keep at least some of her old identity to fall back on. So now she had no back-up strategy. No plan B. Nothing.

What would she do now?

Discreetly, Brandon checked his watch again while shaking hands with the ambassador and her husband. In her heavily accented English, Madame Ambassador asked to have Caroline pointed out to extend her best wishes. Brandon wished he could oblige.

Instead, he caught Jack's attention and motioned him over. Making his lawyer shoulder some of the host duties might wipe that scowl off his face or at least keep him from doing physical harm to Ursula's date.

Jack came escorting Maggie. She shouldn't really be on her feet, but she had insisted for the hundredth time that she was pregnant, not ill. Brandon could strangle the father of her child, if only she would reveal his name.

Brandon introduced Maggie to Madame Ambassador, making sure he emphasized Maggie was his employee, not his wife, especially with her huge baby bulge front and center.

He set Jack to watching over Maggie and helping her introduce the ambassador to the other guests, a function that always worked better in pairs.

Speaking of pairs, where was Caroline? This was the reason he'd married her, to help him schmooze his business relationships.

That gave him pause. When had he lost perspective? He hadn't thought about his reasons for this charade of a marriage since he'd said "I do."

When had it stopped feeling like a sham?

Caroline had shown him that life could be so much more. She had learned to make eggs Benedict for him. She worried over whether he worked too hard and whether he played enough. She rubbed the knot in the back of his neck when he had a headache. And she stirred up her own brand of sexual awareness that made him feel so alive that his nerve endings prickled just thinking about her.

If only she wasn't a virgin. Without all the responsibility and emotional involvement that should go with being a woman's first lover, they could share all the benefits of a happy marriage. But she deserved a lifetime of happiness with the man of her dreams. Not just a few months' worth with the man of her checkbook.

As he thought of that imagined future lover who would initiate Caroline into the world of pleasure between a man and a woman, jealousy clenched his stomach.

Right now, commitment beyond their contract didn't

seem as dire as losing her.

Judge Riley sauntered up to him. "Nice party. Where's the little lady? She's not standing you up like you did the other one, is she? Wouldn't that be ironic?"

"She'll be down shortly." Brandon snagged a champagne flute from a passing tray and put it in the judge's hand.

He gave it back. "I don't drink this girly stuff. But I wouldn't mind a glass of some of that whiskey you were pouring to celebrate your wedding."

Brandon took the glass back and drank it down himself. "You don't know what you're missing." It *was* good champagne.

Caroline might not be very visible, but her planning skills were evident everywhere. The waitstaff was unobtrusive, the food interesting and easy to eat while conversing, and the bartenders were top shelf. He had no idea if the band was any good. Their set wouldn't begin until he and Caroline were ready for the first dance.

The judge licked his lips. "Maybe I will try—"

"If you'll excuse me, I see someone I must speak to."

He did a quick scan, looking for someone—anyone—and spotted Ursula wearing some kind of vintage thing, yellow like lemon meringue pie. Suitable, but quirky, just like her. At least the quirky part.

He wished Jack the best. Give Brandon a traditional woman like Caroline any day. Steady and stable. Whenever he was near her, he felt anchored and calm. Except for his unsatisfied libido, that is. Where the hell was she?

As the judge shifted from one foot to the other, Brandon headed toward Ursula. His investigation of her had turned up nothing so far. A very suspicious nothing. Keeping an eye on her would be a wise action to take.

She was scrutinizing one of the large portraits that had been a new addition when he arrived home.

Major points for Caroline in the decorating department. She might not be the most punctual of people, but she had certainly turned his house into a place he looked forward to coming home to.

Ursula turned to him and smiled. "Great party."

"Thanks. Where's your date?" Brandon searched the crowd, relaxing when he saw Jack occupied with a client.

"He saw an old friend." Ursula gestured with her martini glass toward the governor and a senator.

"He's into politics?"

She smirked. "Alex is into everything."

"You don't sound too happy about that."

She shrugged off his remark and turned the conversation. "I was admiring the paintings Caroline brought down from your attic."

Brandon studied the portrait. "Arrogant fellow, wasn't he?"

"Obviously an ancestor."

"Why do you think so?"

"You're serious? You can't see it? You could be twins." She gestured toward the mirror. "Look."

Brandon looked at his own image in the mirror and back to the portrait on the wall. Yes, he could see similarities in the shape of the eyes and the line of the jaw. He felt lighter as the weight of doubt he'd always carried fell from his shoulders. One more thing Caroline had given him, his heritage.

"He *must* be a relative," Ursula insisted.

"My great-uncle on my grandmother's side. He built this house for his wife."

"Speaking of wives, I've been wondering where yours is?"

"Join the club."

"Is there room for them, too?" Ursula looked pointedly at the older couple who had just entered the house. He was tall and rangy with a harried look on his face. She was petite with Caroline's eyes.

His wife's parents, no doubt.

"Oh!" Ursula jumped.

"What's wrong?"

She pulled her vibrating cell phone from her bosom, flipped it open, and read the text message. "It's Caroline."

"I thought you didn't carry a cell phone."

"Only for emergencies."

"Emergencies?" Brandon's whole body geared up for a rescue. "Is there a problem?"

She patted his arm patronizingly. "It's a girl thing. Is your back door unlocked?"

"Yes, for the caterers."

"Great. Be back in a bit."

She bustled past him, running up the stairs, fluffy yellow dress and all.

Alone, Brandon prepared to meet the in-laws.

Chapter Eleven

A knock sounded on the bedroom door, and Caroline called through the heavy paneling, "Who is it?" as she silently chanted, *Please don't let it be Brandon. Please don't let it be Brandon.*

Ursula's muffled voice came through. "It's me."

Caroline wrapped her robe around her and threw open the door. "This—this..." She held up the dress, hyperventilating. "It's supposed to be my vamp dress."

Ursula took it from her. "Very nice. Looks like it should do the job. Problem?"

Caroline took a deep breath. "It doesn't fit. The seamstress took it up too much."

Ursula held up the dress against her own elegant chiffon masterpiece. Her hair was twisted into a classy French knot that showed off her deep décolletage and her strand of sparkling crystals to their best advantage. She transformed from flowerchild to Princess Grace of Monaco very well.

Caroline collected herself enough to compliment her friend. "You look very nice."

Ursula spread her arms wide and twirled for review.

"Not bad for an artist who lives in an attic, huh?"

Then she took a long look at Caroline. "I've got something that will work for you. You're a bit shorter than me, so you'll have to go with very high heels."

"I don't have any here. I never moved over all my things from my apartment."

Ursula gave her a long knowing look then got back to business. "Shoe size?"

Caroline told her and was relieved that Ursula wore only a half size larger.

"They'll do in a pinch and not even pinch!" Ursula joked, and Caroline forced a smile. "You sit and practice some calming deep breathing and I'll be right back. Sometimes these things happen for a reason, you know?"

Caroline didn't know. All she knew was that she had a house full of the most influential people Brandon knew, and she was upstairs in her bra and panties while he went solo.

The minutes ticked by, stretching endlessly, and Caroline started to itch. *Please don't let it be hives.*

Finally, she heard a small knock.

"Ursula?"

"Yes, it's me."

Caroline opened her door, and Ursula rushed in with a garment bag and shoe box. "These will be just perfect. I bought them at an estate sale but then had to admit to myself that I was just too big boned for the dress."

Caroline shook her head at Ursula. "You're tall and willowy. Not big boned at all." Although right now, she was red faced and glistening with perspiration as her gorgeous lemon chiffon wilted around her, the sign of a true friend.

"But I'm not tiny enough to fit in a teacup like you are." She shoved the bag at Caroline. "I ran all the way. I need to catch my breath." She dramatically fell across Caroline's bed, flinging her arm over her forehead.

"I'm so sorry to put you to so much trouble."

"No trouble at all," she gasped. "Incidents like this make a party memorable."

"This is one party I'll never forget. That's for sure." Caroline worked the zipper of the bag loose. "How's the crowd? Are my parents here yet?"

"You've got a full house. They were coming in the front as I was heading upstairs."

Just great. Brandon would have to meet them without her. This evening was not going as planned at all.

Caroline caught a glimpse of the dress. Red. Scarlet red.

"What do you think?" Ursula propped herself up on her elbows. "Stunning, huh?"

"Yes. Very." Caroline was indeed stunned. She had never worn such a bold color in her entire life.

The slinky fabric slithered as Caroline took it off the hanger. A high, round neckband held up a full halter top. Modest enough, except for the slit from neck to navel. Still, the front was full enough that she would only show sneak-a-boo peeks on occasion. The slim skirt wouldn't have been walkable without the deep front slit that climbed to midthigh. But the back, well, there was no back.

"You'll have to take off that bra and liberate the girls."

"I figured that out." Since she wore bras more for convention than necessity, she could live with that. But carrying off this dress would take a lot more chutzpah than going braless.

Caroline stepped into the connecting bath and wriggled into it. The shimmering scarlet made her skin glow and her brown hair have silky highlights. The back of the dress made a deep, graceful V all the way down to the base of her spine, leaving her whole back exposed.

She felt different. Sexy. She might not be the flash-and-dash kind like Laurel, but she could certainly pull off come-hither sensuality.

The shoes raised her up on her tiptoes, giving her three and a half more inches of height and that sensuous way of walking that only stilettos could provide.

"Let me see," called Ursula from the bedroom. "Will it do?"

"I think so." Caroline joined Ursula and pirouetted. "What do you think?"

"Honey, it's a good thing you've got a big strong husband to keep the men a bay. You're going to drive them crazy." She shoved off the bed looking no worse the wear from her earlier sprint. Not even a hairpin needed readjusting. "Now let me redo your makeup. You'll need more color with this dress."

"You play the piano, tend bar, *and* do makeup? You're a talented woman."

"Theater training." She turned Caroline away from the mirror and dug into her meager supply of cosmetics. In short order, Ursula announced her done.

When Caroline checked the mirror, she saw a woman who could have been featured on the front cover of *Cosmo*. She examined her kohl-lined eyes, ruby-red lips and cheekbones that had never been there before. Ursula took the earrings from her own ears, a dangle of sparkle, dipped them in alcohol, then handed them to Caroline. "A wedding present from me."

"Thanks." Caroline sniffled as her eyes watered with emotion.

"Don't you dare cry. Goth mascara streaks are not part of your look." Ursula handed her a tissue. "Ready?"

A wave of uncertainty hit Caroline. Who was she to pull off this dress? This look? This farce of a marriage?

Ursula put her hand on Caroline's shoulder. "Oh no you don't, girlfriend. Stand up straight. Chin up. You can do this. You just need to keep the proper attitude.

"Attitude." Caroline squared her shoulders.

"It's all about the attitude. Now go vamp your man." She gave Caroline an air kiss. "This must be how mother birds feel. Now do me proud, little redbird."

Caroline stood at the top of the stairway gathering her courage. The Grande Hall was filled shoulder to shoulder, and she could only guess the other rooms would be, too.

Despite the crowd, Brandon was easy to pick out. He was, by far, the most handsome man in the room. He stood with her parents, listening and nodding intently, but suddenly he froze. He turned on his heels and looked straight up the stairway—at her.

His expression darkened so quickly that Caroline almost did an about-face. But Ursula leaned in close.

"You've impressed the man."

"More like angered the man."

"Girlfriend, don't you know the difference between anger and desire?"

Without her volition, her gaze traveled downward. Against all possibility, his expression grew even darker.

"Good shot, Caroline. You vamp well."

"I didn't mean to."

"I guess you're just a natural." Ursula clapped her hands, startling Caroline. "Ladies and gentlemen, may I present Mrs. Brandon D'Estrehan."

Applause broke out all around. Caroline had to concentrate to keep her head up as she descended the stairs. She could feel the split in her dress opening and closing with each step, could feel Brandon watching that flash of thigh, and let a smile creep onto her lips.

He met her at the bottom of the stairs, held out his hand for hers and kissed it. His mouth on her delicate skin sent fireworks up her arm. "What's the Mona Lisa smile about?"

"That's a secret between me and Mona." She reclaimed her hand before it burst into flames. "Sorry I'm late."

"Definitely worth the wait."

Her parents joined them, her mother looking pleased, but her father appearing a bit grey with brackets around his mouth.

Still, her father said, "It seems you've found yourself a good man, Caroline."

"So it would seem, Dad."

Brandon quirked an eyebrow at her answer. She gave him a wink and watched while his pupils darkened. Vamping was very heady stuff.

Her mother hugged her and whispered, "Your eyes light up when you look at him. He seems very special to you. You love him, don't you?"

Without hesitation, Caroline whispered back, "He is. And yes, I do." She felt the conviction in her own voice all the way to her soul. When had it happened? When had she fallen in love with Brandon?

Was it the first moment she saw him? Did she really believe in love at first site? Yes, she did. Unequivocably.

Brandon held out his hand for her. "The band is waiting for us to dance the first dance."

"In these?" She took a step forward to show off her shoes, exposing most of her leg. "You'll have to hold me close."

His voice deepened into a growl. "I promised I wouldn't let you fall, remember?"

A hazy memory became clearer. "That's right. On our wedding day. I believed you. I still do."

She took his hand to pull him to the designated dance floor near the entry doors but came to an abrupt stop when he didn't move. She knew the minute he caught sight of the back of her dress. He drew in his breath as he pulled her back toward him.

"Where's the rest of your dress?"

"Pardon?" Mona Lisa didn't have anything on her tonight.

"The back. It's missing."

"You like it?"

"Too much." He glared around him. "Nobody else better like it, though. Don't you need a wrap of some sort?"

"Oh, no. Dancing always makes me *hot*."

Instead of answering, Brandon stepped into the open doorway of the Rose Room and signaled the orchestra. They broke into a rousing rendition of a Louis Armstrong favorite, and Brandon competently led her into an old-fashioned swing.

With his hands holding her, keeping her balanced, her heels didn't bother her at all, but his hand on her bare back bothered her a lot. "You're very good."

"My grandmother was a Grande Dame for one of the local cotillions. She made me take dancing lessons for a while. And you?"

"I went to Cabrini High School. We learned ballroom dancing in physical education classes and danced in the gym every rainy day."

"Isn't that an all-girls school?"

Even though she'd danced for years, she had to count momentarily to stay in step before answering. "Yes, it is."

"Who led?"

"The taller girls had to, so never me." She saw her father nearby. "And now I think it's my dad's turn to dance with me."

"Stand still a moment." He positioned her in front of him.

"Why?"

"I need a moment to think of God and country before I can walk you over there."

Caroline glanced downward.

"Don't look." He lifted her chin. "You'll only make it worse."

She made a deliberate investigation of him, top to toe, not helping his cause at all.

"Tease," he called her. His dimple softened his grin. He led her through the crowd, stopping to motion to a passing waiter. "What can I get you?"

"Orange juice, virgin," Caroline answered."

"Not drinking tonight?"

"The last time I drank, I ended up married."

She expected him to laugh. Instead, his brows drew together in worry. He leaned in so close his breath tickled her neck. To their guests, he must look like he was whispering romantic intimacies. "Has it been so bad?"

That stopped her in her tracks. "No. No, it's not been bad at all. In fact, I think these last two weeks have been the best ones in my life so far."

He let out a breath. "Good. There's more to come."

"I'm looking forward to it." She let her fingers trail down his arm. "Just the two of us."

The waiter behind them cleared his throat. Obviously, he needed a bit more training. But the mood was broken.

Brandon leaned down and gave her a kiss on the cheek. "One for the guests?"

She wanted to protest that her words had been for him and him alone, but there was the nosey waiter to consider. Instead, he handed Brandon a drink from his tray and promised to return soon with her juice.

Meanwhile, Brandon led her over to her father, who was watching them with a pained look on his face. "Impulsiveness isn't like you, Caroline. But it seems to suit you. You certainly seem to be taken by your young man."

"And he's taken with her." Brandon interjected. "But

right now, he's looking for her mother to dance with."

"I guess that's my cue for our father-daughter dance." He stood and held out his hand for his daughter. "How about asking the band for a slow one. My dancing shoes haven't had enough practice lately for a fox trot or a rumba."

"Sure, Dad." Caroline caught the band leader's attention and signaled for a slower song. He wrapped up the big band arrangement and played a bluesy number, perfect for a slow two step. From the corner of her eye, she watched her mother dance with Brandon. By her mother's expression, her husband was exuding his famous charisma.

"You seem to be happy, Caroline."

"I am, Daddy." She had been worried for nothing. She was telling the absolute truth. "Brandon's a wonderful man."

"We were concerned about his reputation and the quickness of this marriage."

"I'm just like you, Dad. Slow to deliberate, but once I know what I want, I don't hesitate."

He chuckled at that. "You've got me there. Once I decided to marry your mother, we eloped the next day."

"I guess this apple didn't fall far from the tree." She leaned in to kiss his cheek. "You made a good bargain, Dad. I think I did, too."

As the song ended, her father said he wanted to take a look at Brandon's business library and wandered off in that direction.

Claiming best man privileges, Jack led her into the next dance. He wasn't as smooth as Brandon, but that could have been because he spent all his time glaring at Ursula and her date. Before he permanently damaged her toes, she urged him to cut in. "Go on. Ask her. She won't make a scene by refusing you."

"That's what I want." His sarcasm was thick. "A woman who chooses me over a messy alternative." Still, he led them next to Ursula and tapped on her date's shoulder.

"May I cut in?"

The man looked as if he would hesitate until Caroline forced the issue. "I would love you to show me that move you and Ursula just did." She held out her hand to him and he reluctantly took it.

They never got to try the step. He introduced himself as Alex as he spun her around, right into Brandon. Without being asked, Alex handed her over, muttering something about spiking the punch bowl.

The music sounded brighter as she twirled in Brandon's arms.

"That guy had his hands all over you. He was lucky I cut in when I did."

Caroline didn't bother to point out that Alex had only touched her palm with one hand and the back of her shoulder with the other. Nor did she mention that under Alex's touch, she felt nothing, while Brandon's elicited shock waves down her spine.

Maybe she should. Maybe she should just blurt out that she'd changed her mind and ask which side of the bed he wanted.

Subtleness wasn't working. She had caressed Brandon every chance she got, but she had felt like she was trying to tame a wild cat, and she meant tiger not tabby.

He'd jumped at first. Now, he didn't pull away when she straightened his collar or touched his arm. In fact, he seemed to lean into her now. Last night, when he'd held her hand, she thought she would do cartwheels.

If tonight was going to be the night, she needed to take action.

Just as she talked herself into being so bold, the song came to an end, and Caroline was called away to join Ursula and a woman who often graced the covers of the local society pages.

She would have stayed for another dance, but Brandon urged her to join them. "The sooner you make the rounds, the sooner everyone will go home."

Was he thinking along the same lines as she was? He ran his hand down her back before telling her, "Go. Go, before I can't let you go."

Caroline looked into his eyes, trying to find a hidden meaning, but he was turning away from her, and she didn't call him back.

Ursula was saying, "Weddings Divine is alive and well. I'm sure Caroline would love to give you a quote on your daughter's wedding. Wouldn't you, Caroline?"

"I would have thought, with your marriage to Brandon D'Estrehan, that you wouldn't want to work any more. After all, you're not a single woman any longer, are you?" The socialite had perfected the art of saying one thing and meaning another.

"Weddings Divine isn't work. It's been my dream for a long time."

The woman gave her an assessing look. "I understand you put together this party yourself. Very nice. I hadn't heard of you before, well, before that other wedding that didn't happen."

Caroline had expected cattiness like this. Still, she had a business to grow.

"Thank you. I'd love to discuss the details with you and your daughter. I'm only scheduling a select few brides to work with. If you want to set up an appointment with me, call soon. Now if you'll excuse me."

She gave a regal nod and headed toward her mother and Maggie chatting under the newly hung portraits.

Ursula followed her over. "You aren't really considering taking on her daughter's wedding, are you?"

Caroline grinned. "Her daughter may need an advocate. And right now, I'm not teeming with prospects."

Ursula shrugged. "You'd better charge her for the trouble, then."

Under the portrait of Brandon's ancestor, her mother was saying, "I knew within days that I was pregnant. Breast tenderness, sleepiness, the need to be held and cuddled."

Maggie was nodding her understanding. "Crying jags. I've never cried so much in my entire life as the first three months I was pregnant." She gave Caroline a wink. "If you want to see Brandon blanch, break out in tears in front of him."

Caroline remembered the tears she hadn't been able to hold back at their first meeting. Her tears hadn't seemed to affect him at all as he drove his bargain home. He'd used her emotional vulnerability to seal the deal, and she'd ended up right where he wanted her. Married to him. But now that she could read the signs, would she see him in a new light?

"I'm not much for tears, but I'll remember that." She could go for whole hours at a time forgetting theirs was a business contract, until she came across conversations like these to remind her that first and foremost, Brandon was a businessman. Albeit, a very sexy one.

Still, not much chance of pregnancy with Brandon, not with that prenuptial clause in place. She could never bring a child into a marriage that had an expiration date. And she would never, ever give up her child.

From across the room, she saw her husband joining the senator and Ursula's date. A tall, willowy blonde she hadn't yet met intruded on their circle, brushing against Brandon's arm. Caroline had to take a deep breath to keep from charging over there and ejecting their guest.

This may only be business, but hopefully she could turn it into business with fringe benefits. Maybe it was time to join her husband and let him have another look at her dress.

Maggie must have picked up on her reluctance to talk babies. "For Monday, I've got three new interviews lined up for your personal assistant."

Caroline sighed. "Okay. Maybe we'll find one that's compatible." She explained to her mother and Ursula. "The women are either too eager and in awe of working with the wife of Brandon D'Estrehan or they were drill sergeants in their former lives."

Maggie patted her stomach. "I've been doing double duty, but your schedule has been nonexistent so far. You're about to be very busy, and I'll be a bit too busy soon, myself."

"I'll do it," Ursula said. "I'll be your PA until you find a permanent one."

Caroline ignored the frown Maggie sent her way. "Hired."

Without turning, she knew Brandon approached by the prickle down her spine. He wrapped his arm around her shoulders and leaned in close.

Brandon hated to be the bearer of bad news. He braced himself for any reaction, not sure how his new wife and her mother would handle his message.

"Caroline, your father isn't feeling well. I've called an ambulance."

But both Caroline and her mother were made of sterner stuff.

"What's wrong?" Caroline asked through stiff lips.

Brandon could see the activity behind her eyes as she assessed his every nuance. The way she studied people, she would make a very good poker player.

"He's feeling dizzy and has shortness of breath. One of the guests who is a doctor has given him an aspirin and he's resting in my office."

"Heart attack?"

"Maybe."

Caroline's mother blinked, then started making decisions. "I'll get my purse and be ready when the ambulance gets here. You'll find me in your office until then."

Caroline turned to Ursula. "Your first duty as my PA is to take care of our guests."

"Will do, boss."

Brandon took charge, for which Caroline was grateful. "Caroline, I'll bring the car around and we'll follow the ambulance in. Maggie, please make my excuses to the guests."

"Thanks. Brandon, I'm going to wait in your office with Dad until the emergency personnel get here."

Her father lay on the couch assuring everyone he was all right, even though his face was the color of paste. A woman in Christian Dior leaned over him with her fingers pressed to his jugular, counting pulses while her mother held his hand.

"Caroline, I'm so sorry to interrupt your party."

Caroline shushed him. "You're more important than a party, Dad."

Caroline didn't have to wait long.

No siren sounded, but through the windows the red strobe of the ambulance lights sprayed color across the room then washed it out again as it parked in front.

Within seconds, the paramedics rushed in with their gurney, clearing the path.

Brandon took Caroline's hand, and his comfort wrapped her like a blanket. "I've got the car out front. Let's get out of their way so they can do their job."

As the paramedics swung open the door, a stiff wind blew out all the candles in the Hall. The high humidity carried the scent of imminent rain.

One of the paramedics escorted her mother into the ambulance alongside her father. Rain pelted them as they ran for the car.

The cardiac waiting room had a half-dozen people sitting dazed in chairs as they waited for news. She and Brandon joined them. Soon, her mother came in, too. They received reports of tests being run with promises of updates. The rest was a blur of more tests and more waiting as minutes stretched into the wee hours of the morning.

Sometime around two, Brandon trailed his finger across her cheek, awakening her. She pulled his coat tighter around her and sat up straight in the stiff chair, abruptly aware of where she was and why.

Her mother was crying, and Brandon had his arms around both of them.

"Is he…?"

"Fine." Her mother said through her tears. "He's fine."

Caroline looked to Brandon for answers. "Your father took some over-the-counter air-sickness medication that interacted with his high blood pressure medicine. They have him stabilized now. No heart attack. No permanent harm done."

"They're moving him to a regular room tonight, but they expect to release him in the morning. I'm going to stay with him tonight, and we'll catch a cab back home tomorrow," Caroline's mother said. "Why don't you two go home and get some rest. With this weather, the sooner you're both safe, the better I'll rest."

Brandon nodded his agreement. "Call us if you need us."

"I will." She kissed Caroline on the cheek. "You chose well, daughter. He's a special man."

"I think so, too." Caroline meant it from the bottom of her heart. And soon, she would show him how special he was.

Chapter Twelve

Sheets of rain kept visibility to a few inches. Streets ran like rivers. The car shook form the force of the wind as they pulled up to Brandon's office building, the closest place of refuge. The long drive in the storm was a risk they didn't need to take.

Wind tore Caroline's umbrella from her hands. Her hair immediately plastered to her head, and her borrowed dress would never recover.

Brandon grabbed her hand and pulled her against the wind. "Hold on to me," he shouted over the downpour.

Without his strength, Caroline would have gone sprawling beneath the wind's assault. She had no intention of letting go.

They crowded together in the building's alcove as he punched in the security code for the door, his body protecting her from the brunt of the storm.

They were both soaked through by the time the door opened. Despite the muggy heat, she started to shiver on the elevator ride up to his penthouse.

"Cold?" Brandon wrapped his arms around her, his body

heat steamy against her clamminess.

"Partly." She leaned into him. "Partly the aftereffects of nerves, I think."

"You've had a long evening."

"Yes." She turned in his arms so they were face-to-face. "Thanks for being my rock." She raised on tiptoe and planted a kiss on his lips.

Every cell in Brandon's body responded to that kiss. She wrapped her arms around his neck and pulled him down to her. His coat fell to the floor, leaving her back bare to entice his touch.

His resistance was too eroded to hold back his response. His mouth explored hers as his hands traced down her spine. Passion arced between them, making the air thick with wanting.

He wanted to take her right there on the floor of the elevator. But his security watched and recorded every move from the motion-activated cameras, and he doubted that voyeurism was her style. It certainly wasn't his.

The thought of someone else seeing the languid passion in her eyes made him crazy.

Using the last dregs of his willpower, he broke off their kiss. "Caroline. Cameras."

She looked up at him and blinked as if she was coming out of a trance. Then she smiled that Mona Lisa smile. Her body dragged along his as she slowly let herself down from her tiptoes. Did his little innocent know she was playing with fire? Did she want this to end up in his bed?

And then what? In her naiveté, she didn't know how to play the game of recreational sex. She didn't know the rules like an experienced woman would and wouldn't know how to end the game with both of them winners. And he never wanted her to learn the heartache of losing.

As the elevator slowed, Brandon shoved his hands in his

pockets when that was the last place he wanted them. Of course, he'd used the cameras as an excuse. What if he did finish this seduction? Where would they be tomorrow with her expectations and his regrets?

If he knew anything about his wife, he knew she wasn't the type of woman who used sex as recreation. That's one of the things he lov-admired about her. Not love. Love was something other people shared.

Love didn't come with a hasty wedding to a stranger and a prenuptial contract based on a six-month marriage agreement.

Right now, their business merger was working out better than he had hoped for. Who could predict the same for a personal merger? Was he willing to give up this relationship for a night of sex?

Was there a way to make it something more?

Finally, the elevator stopped at the penthouse, and the doors opened into the foyer. With the loft-like floor plan, most of the apartment was exposed as the doors slid open and he saw his apartment through Caroline's eyes.

It was the perfect man cave. Big leather furniture. Bigger flat screen TV with surround sound and a newspaper spread across the coffee table. His housekeeper knew better than to move anything he left out. She had her instructions to dust around things.

"You decorated this yourself, didn't you?"

"Does my lack of taste show?"

"No. Your personality."

He wondered what the unusual painting of Blue Dog by New Orleans native George Rodrigue said about him.

When a shiver shook Caroline, he turned his attention to her, wrapped in his coat and sopping wet.

"I'm afraid I'm dripping on your hardwood floor," she apologized.

"It's seen worse. But you need to get warmed up." He would have liked to offer his body heat, but stuck with something safer—for both of them. "My shower's right down the hall through the bedroom."

Caroline wanted to stop along the way and examine Brandon's penthouse in detail, but she was freezing in her wet clothes. "A shower sounds divine."

Heavy water pressure pummeled and massaged the aches and stresses from her shoulder blades that the party and the hospital had put there. But the water couldn't give her any relief from the sexual awareness that kept her on edge around her husband.

Now was the time. She had a decision to make. She would not only be giving him her virginity, she would be giving him her heart to hold. And it had no six-month escape clause like her prenuptial contract.

'Tis better to have loved and lost than never to have loved at all. It had been one of her favorite quotes, until she found herself having to test it.

With great reluctance, she finished up her shower, knowing Brandon would want one, too. And tonight she wanted him satisfied. More plainly stated, she wanted to satisfy him.

He was the one. No amount of walking around it would change the way she felt.

While Caroline rifled through his closet, she deliberated over the right words to say. Blurting out *Let's have sex* would probably do the trick. She doubted Brandon would be opposed to the idea. But she wasn't sure she could say the words. At least Audrey Hepburn had screenwriters who put the words in her mouth for her.

Caroline had a new appreciation for all those in the dating world. Initiating lovemaking was risky business, full of possibilities for rejection if she said the wrong thing at the wrong time.

Finally, she choose a crisp white, button-down shirt for her seduction scheme. The tail hung several inches past her derriere and the sleeves needed to be rolled up a dozen times to free her hands. She started buttoning at the base of her breastbone downward, wishing for more cleavage.

Borrowing a pair of Brandon's running socks to keep her feet warm was practical, if not sexy. The footwear was not the most attractive, but she didn't need cold feet de facto while she fought off a case of cold feet in spirit.

In a spurt of shyness, she wrapped herself in a heavy robe big enough to go around her twice. It still had tags dangling from the sleeve. Obviously, he'd never worn it. She knew he was more the gym shorts, type. Or maybe, in private, he wore nothing at all.

She had a hard time imagining him naked without blushing, but imagine him, she did. Soon, she wouldn't have to rely on her own creativity. Soon, she would know what he looked like sans clothes. He already knew what she looked like au naturel so she was behind in this spread.

She should say it. Just say, *I want your body. Now.* Or at least get rid of the robe.

Instead, she said, "Your turn," as she passed him and headed for the smell of coffee.

Caroline heard the shower start and wished she were the type of woman who could strip and join him. But she wasn't. Not yet, anyway.

And why not? She questioned herself. Was it belated shyness, or extreme modesty?

No. It was fear. Fear of rejection. Fear of caring too much. Fear of what comes next.

Caroline meandered around Brandon's apartment, getting a clearer idea of the man. He'd lit candles and hurricane lamps all over the place as a precaution since the lights kept flickering and a blackout seemed inevitable.

A photo of an older couple sat in a frame on a side table. Paperback novels by James Lee Burke were stacked on that same table. When she heard the shower shut off, she scooted out of his bedroom and headed for the less personal kitchen. She was examining the bare pantry when the lights went out.

The aura of the candles and lamps cast the apartment in moving shadows.

"Caroline," Brandon called from his bedroom, "Are you all right?"

A good femme fatale would have a witty, sexy comeback. "I'm fine," was all she managed. She did find the courage to discard the concealing robe, though. With no air conditioning, she could always explain it away as the room heating up. Witty phrases like *plenty of electricity between us* and *too much body heat* popped into her head. Maybe she could work those into some kind of repartee?

She made her way to his dining room table where two lamps cast twin circles of light on the wooden surface.

Brandon emerged form the bedroom carrying a blanket and pillow. "You must be exhausted. I'll bed down on the couch so you can rest."

She should say something about the bed being big enough for both of them. Maybe a throaty suggestion that she didn't need much room if she lay on top of him. But her throat clogged.

In a clinch, she said the first thing that popped into her head. "I'm not really tired right now. Actually, I'm feeling a bit restless." Not bad. A bit subtle, but not bad.

"All right." Brandon looked down at the blanket in his hands, then back at her as if he'd played his last card and waited for her to show her hand.

He walked to the windows that looked out over the Mississippi River, but the only view tonight was the reflection of the room behind him.

Brandon watched Caroline pace the living room like a caged cat. She was restless. Storms did that to some people, brought out the elemental in them. Even in the ghostly reflection, Caroline looked sexy as hell. She wore his shirt better than it had ever been worn before. Her legs looked so long and lean beneath the curved hem. Even his socks, puddled around her ankles, looked enticing, as if he should be pulling them off, one at a time and running his hand up her calf, up her thigh, up…

Damn, he wanted her. If only…

Was she willing to…?

Relationship. That was the thought he kept skirting around. Not a business partnership but a personal one. *Life everlasting, amen.* Well, maybe not that long.

Then how long?

The thought of not being with Caroline any time in the future, near or far, seemed unfeasible. Intolerable. Excruciatingly empty.

He turned to pour himself a drink from the brandy decanter on the occasional table near the window.

"Want one?"

"I can't. I'm still taking antibiotics for my sniffles."

"Right." He made his a double.

Caroline came up behind him and looked out, but her eyes followed his reflection in the glass. "Why don't we play poker? Care for a tournament?"

"Sure. You know how?" Anything for a distraction. "I'm not a card shark, but I've played before."

Brandon retrieved a deck of cards from a drawer and gestured toward the table. "Lady's choice."

In the lamp's glow, Caroline's brown eyes sparkled. "Strip poker. Five card stud. I'll deal."

Strip poker? Did that mean what he thought it meant?

She cocked an eyebrow at him. There was nothing naive in that tempting look she gave him.

Oh, yeah. That's what it meant.

He knew he had a slew of excuses and best intentions, but he had exhausted his supply of common sense.

Brandon considered his gym shorts and T-shirt and her socks and shirt. He'd bet money she had on nothing underneath it. This could be a short tournament. He would do his best to see that they both came out winners in the end.

Caroline handled the cards competently, shuffling and dealing, but she didn't have a poker face. Even in the dim light, her body language broadcast her happiness or sadness with each card and telegraphed what her next move would be.

In her first round, she lost a sock. Then, he had a lousy hand and lost his shirt. He could only hope the same would eventually happen to her.

"Losing suits you." Caroline licked her lips, and he almost threw in the cards right then and there. But he liked this pace she was leading him along. This was the best foreplay he'd ever had.

He put all the concentration he could muster into his game but still lost one of his own socks.

On the next hand, Caroline lost her other sock. When she lost the next hand, she yanked the top button off his shirt. What was she doing? Whatever it was, he liked it.

Another three buttons and the shirt was defying gravity by staying closed.

He lost another sock and was down to shorts alone. Of course, she wouldn't know that he went commando at night. Thanks goodness there was nothing between him and the open air but those shorts. Right now, either boxers or briefs would have cramped his style in the most painful of ways.

This would be the last deal. She flipped the cards between them. He could tell by her eyes that she had a great hand.

Deliberately, she took one of her cards from her hand and held it up. "Just one. How about you?"

He looked at his measly pair of threes. "I'll hang onto these." He was sure to lose.

He prepared to brace himself for being at her mercy. Not an unappealing proposition at all.

She dealt herself another card. Every move she made signaled her winning hand. She faked a frown and bit at a fingernail. Then she stacked her cards one on top of the other.

"That's it. I fold. You win."

She threw the game for him?

She threw the game for him!

"Aren't you going to tell me to take it off?"

"Take it off." His voice sounded rough, parched, like he'd been days without water. No, not water. Love. He was thirsting for love, dying for love. Caroline's love.

When had it happened? When had he given her his heart?

She stood and his buttonless shirt gaped open on her. What the hell did it matter when it happened? All that was important right now was what was about to happen.

She shrugged off the shirt and let it fall to the ground. "I guess it's time for bed now. But I'm a bit chilly. Want to warm me?"

Words deserted Brandon as he picked her up and carried her to his bed. He put her down as gently as if she'd been a demitasse china cup. She was so small, so delicate.

"Come here, big boy." That didn't sound delicate at all.

She was his and his alone. "Protection?" Logic was quickly leaving him. He barely got the words out.

"Birth control."

He nodded his comprehension and peeled off his shorts, then caged her, supporting himself on all fours. "You're stunning."

"So are you."

"I want you."

"Me, too." Then she reached out and ran her fingernail down his chest. "I've been wanting to do that ever since you took off your shirt."

He leaned down and kissed her breast, worshipping her nipple with his tongue. "And I've been wanting to do that ever since I undressed you."

"The other one is jealous."

"We can't have that, can we."

She was so sexy. She knew just how to handle him. He gave equal attention to her other breast.

She grabbed him on either side of his face and made him look at her, directly into her eyes. In the candle glow, he saw the passion shining through the windows of her soul.

Her whisper demanded, "Now. Inside me now."

"Yes." He caressed her all the way down her body before fitting himself to her. "So tight."

Obligingly, she lifted her legs and wrapped them around his hips. "Better?"

Despite her wetness, her entrance was so unyielding. Just as he suspected. "Caroline, we've got to go slow. You're a—"

Oh, no. He wasn't pulling back now. He was the one. Caroline took control as she felt the flame deep inside her build into a conflagration that could not be contained. All those nights reading *Cosmo* were coming in very handy.

"Flip us."

"Pardon?"

"Flip us. Put me on top."

"Yes, ma'am." And it was done.

"You're good at everything you do, aren't you?"

"Thanks." He grinned up at her, then frowned at her natural resistance. "Go slow, sweetheart. Just ease dow—"

Before he could finish, she plunged downward, forcing the issue. Although the pain took her breath away, she smiled through it, her moment of triumph intact. "Not any more."

But her need to move soon overcame the ache that was quickly fading. She took control of the rhythm, putting her hands on either side of his hips and holding him close when he would have pulled away. "Finish it."

"Yes, ma'am." And finish it, he did.

Brandon kept his movements shallow, even when she urged more. He teased and nibbled at her neck, whispering how beautiful she was, how much he wanted her, how he never wanted to let her go.

Waves and waves of passion pulsed through her, crashed around her, spun her world until she was dizzy with the intensity of the emotions rushing over her.

Brandon roared, the sound primitive and deep, as pleasure throbbed through him. An eternity later, he collapsed beside her, burrowing his face in her nape as he rained kisses on the delicate skin.

Caroline closed her eyes and soaked in the tenderness that followed their combustive lovemaking. Yes, he was special. He was the one she'd been waiting for all her life.

If only it was reciprocal. But making love to Brandon had been completely her decision. She hadn't asked for commitment, and she would be foolish to expect it.

He must have sensed her mood change because he raised up, dropped a teasing kiss on her nose and said, "You're pretty bossy in bed."

"I guess I am. Sorry."

"No, don't apologize. I like it." He skimmed a thumb along her fragile collarbone. "You can always be the boss in my bed."

"I like the sound of that." But how long would always last?

Stop it, Caroline. You will not ruin the moment by this second-guessing. She had tonight, and she planned to make enough memories to last a lifetime.

"Kiss me again."

"Whatever you say, boss." And he did on every inch of her body.

Chapter Thirteen

Caroline awoke the next morning with a strong sense of déjà vu. The pillow next to her was cold, although the scent of Brandon lingered.

The noise in the dining area had her sitting up and clutching her sheet to her naked body. "Brandon?"

He stood in the doorway dressed in a suit and tie. No doubt about it, the man could carry off any look, from designer suit to birthday suit and everything in between.

He held out a sundress and sandals. "I brought these over from the house. I didn't think you'd want to wear my shirt out of here."

"Especially with the buttons missing."

"Especially with…"

She licked her dry lips and gloried in the way his eyes narrowed and darkened. "Thanks. And thanks for last night."

A frown creased his brow. "About last night. You were a virgin."

"Does it matter?"

"Hell yes, it matters." He grabbed the doorframe as if he needed to hold on to it to stay put.

"Good or bad?" She let the sheet slide until it barely covered her breasts.

His eyes followed its downward drift. He blinked to get back on track. "It depends."

Feeling sexy was glorious. She shrugged and the sheet plunged to her waist. "Depends on what?"

"On whether you're happy about it or sad about it."

"Do I look sad?"

"Why'd you do it, Caroline? Why'd you give such a precious gift to me?" In his voice she heard a yearning, a pleading for her answer.

Should she tell him?

"I was waiting for someone special." Caroline took a deep breath and confessed, "I found him. I love you."

Brandon felt like he'd been punched in the gut, or the heart, he wasn't sure which. Is this what commitment felt like? This intensity that felt like an elephant sitting on his heart, making it hard to keep his breathing even?

He wasn't the kind of guy that could do forever. He wanted to be. He wanted to know that every morning began with Caroline and every evening ended with her. Maybe even little Carolines and a little Brandon, too.

But did he have it in him? He didn't know how to be a husband, to be a father. And commitment was too important a job to fail at. When a man failed at being a husband and father, he left all the others in shreds.

He couldn't do that. Shouldn't have done what he did last night. Caroline deserved so much better.

Caroline pulled the covers back up to her neck. "You don't have to say anything. No strings."

"Of course there are strings. You were an innocent."

"Innocent? Are we in a Victorian romance or something? I might have been an *innocent*, but I'm not an *idiot*." She raised up on her knees, letting her covers drop. "And a full-grown woman, as you can see. And I knew full well what I was doing. What I have been trying to do for days now. You're a hard man to seduce, Mr. D'Estrehan. And I mean *hard* in every way you can imagine."

"But our contract…"

"Sex wasn't in our contract. In fact, I remember we left it open as my option. I opted in. And our contract stands exactly as written."

"Caroline, this is serious."

"Only if you make it that way. Nothing needs to change between us." She put his buttonless shirt on. "Brandon, I'm not asking you for anything. I didn't tell you I loved you expecting anything in return. I told you because I do and I wanted you to know. No strings attached."

He had to say it and get it over with. "I'm leaving for Belgium this afternoon."

"The deal you've been working on?"

"It's unraveling fast. You can come with me."

"I don't have a passport." She'd never had reason, never had the opportunity to travel until they married.

He'd known that when he made the offer. A break was just what he needed, what *they* needed. Why then, did he feel like he was betraying a trust she hadn't asked for?

"Business. I've got meetings set up."

"Right. Business." She climbed out of bed. Those glorious legs, those high, firm breasts had him leaning against the doorframe for support.

"I made quite a few contacts last night. I have a feeling Weddings Divine will be picking up, too. And I have a schedule full of charity functions to attend."

"Right. Plenty to keep you busy."

"I think I'll miss you." She walked toward him, grace in every step. "Will you miss me?"

"Yes. Most definitely."

The long plane ride had given Brandon sixteen hours to brood. Sixteen excruciating hours to think of all the ways he could have handled her declaration of love.

Chief among them was saying "I love you" back to her. But he'd never said those words to anyone, and he wasn't sure he knew how.

As the plane waited on the tarmac for their gate so they could disembark, he pulled out his Blackberry. Three times he started a text message to her. And all three times he erased it without sending it.

He could call her, but what would he say at two in the morning, her time? *I love you, too?* But he was a day late with that one. Besides, he wanted the first time he ever said those words to her to be face-to-face.

A driver met him as soon as he cleared customs. He checked his watch. Still too early to call her. He completed his text message. *Arrived safely. Will call later.* And sent it before he could talk himself out of it.

He met with the CEOs of the two companies that should be merging, noting the tension between them as solid as the conference table that separated one side from the other.

The next few hours were filled with talks of broken contracts and disintegrating trust. They argued about implied promises ignored and good faith agreements gone bad. Neither CEO had made progress, too worried that taking a risk would leave him too vulnerable to the other.

As Brandon negotiated through the talks, urging both failing companies to come together as one healthy corporation, to compromise, take risks that the other party would be faithful to their agreements and merge for the good of the employees, he realized he was lecturing himself. Caroline had taken all those risks. She'd compromised and taken chances that he would keep his word. Hell, even their six-month agreement was an uncontracted handshake that she'd taken on faith.

And what had he trusted in? Nothing but the paper between them. Even when she'd made herself most vulnerable, given herself to him with no holding back then telling him she loved him, he'd failed to give even a sliver of his heart in return.

That evening, after his lonely supper in the hotel, he went up to his empty room. This was what life had been before Caroline. No one to care when he came and went. No one to care what his day had been like. No one to care if he was alive or dead.

Before jet lag claimed him, he called her. She answered, her voice groggy. "Hello?"

"It's me. Brandon."

"I recognized the number."

"I just wanted to…" He rubbed his hand across his eyes. "How's your dad?"

"Fine. They flew back yesterday after your plane left."

He searched for something, anything to keep her on the phone. "How was your day?"

"Fine. Just fine." She hesitated. "And yours?"

"Rough. Looks like I'll be over here awhile."

"Oh."

Try as he might, Brandon couldn't read anything in her noncommittal single syllable. "What do you have planned for your day?"

"Weddings Divine business, Baby Cuddlers, and a Support Literacy auction. You'll be making a very nice donation."

"If they have any signed author copies by Louisiana authors, get me copies, please."

"Will do."

Although he was tired, Brandon was reluctant to break the connection. "Sounds like you have a busy day planned."

"And evening. I'll be out late tonight with Ursula, Jack, and Alex. Little theater production."

"Alex? Who's Alex?"

"Ursula's date at our party, remember?"

Yes, he did remember. "Tall, imposing. Chatted up all the politicians."

"That's the one. I think he's a federal attorney of some sort."

In the background, he heard the buzzing of her alarm and then her slap as she silenced it. "I've got to go. The decorator is coming early to discuss the fourth bedroom."

Reluctantly he said, "I'll call you tomorrow, okay?" Getting that glimmer of insight into her day brightened his night.

"Yes, tomorrow." A silence stretched between them. A silence that should have been filled with "I love you." Instead, she said, "No caffeine after six. It keeps you up."

"Right," he agreed as his spirits lifted. Didn't her nagging mean that she still might care?

"Sleep tight," she whispered, then broke the connection.

He cradled the phone between his shoulder and his ear, wishing the connection back. Just like he'd wished for their last time together back to do over again. But he'd wished for a different past enough times in his life to understand the futility of trying to turn back time.

Laying the phone on his nightstand, he dropped his head onto the pillow that didn't smell of Caroline and stared at the ceiling long into the night.

Negotiations were painfully slow with each of the CEOs nitpicking terms and handpicking officers, trying to posture their favorites in the best positions.

He called her after his frustrating day. "If they'd just stick to the contract," he complained to Caroline, "we wouldn't have any problems."

"Contracts spell out everything so there's no room for confusion."

"Exactly. You'd think they'd honor their own agreements, but they're trying to squeeze out every penny they can from this merger. A contract isn't just about a legal, binding agreement, it's about character and pride, too. I need to remind them of that."

"Are you sure it's all about the money?"

"Of course it is. That's what everything is about." He took a deep breath. "I miss talking through these problems with you. They always seem so simple, so cut-and-dried, after we discuss them."

"Glad I could help."

Brandon shrugged his tense shoulders, wishing Caroline was there to rub the knots out. "I wish you were here."

"I miss you, too. Come home soon."

"As soon as I can," he promised.

The following morning, Brandon bought up the majority shares, declared himself CEO, and sent them all packing with bonuses much smaller than they had hoped for.

It had been a while since he had set up a company from the ground up, and he ended up traveling throughout Belgium and France, renewing old acquaintances and sizing up candidates for major positions.

As he traveled, he kept wanting to turn to Caroline and show her his favorite places, take her to his favorite restaurants, and get her opinions on his decisions. He missed her as he had never missed anyone before. More than that, he felt incomplete without her. Breakfasts were bad, but evenings were the worst. He wanted his nasty decaf tea and her hand trailing along his shoulders. He wanted her in his bed. He wanted her, heart, body and soul.

Instead, he had to settle for a hard, cold plastic phone receiver and a few sleepy sentences each night before he fell into bed and she started her new day.

No strings, she'd said. Apparently she'd lassoed his heart.

Two weeks later, he knew he'd been gone too long when Caroline's conversations got shorter and shorter. Brandon intended to fix that the minute he was back on home soil.

Then she stopped picking up the phone.

After three mornings in a row of no communication, he called and called until she answered.

"Hello?" She sounded awful.

"Where have you been?"

"Sleeping in a bit."

He heard crackles and crunching in the background. "Breakfast on the run?"

"Crackers."

"What happened to pancakes and eggs Benedict?"

She groaned. "I'm taking a break from the kitchen."

"You're not skipping meals, are you?"

"Not all meals. Just breakfast." She hesitated. "Brandon, I'm late."

"You're always late. Whoever is waiting on you can wait until you have a decent breakfast."

"I've got to go."

"Talk to you later," he said, but he was talking to a disconnected phone line. He had to get home before his fragile relationship unraveled. Or at least, make it progress far enough along to call it a relationship.

The new company was still shaky, but they would have to sink or swim without him. It seemed his marriage was even shakier.

He called the airport to book reservations on the first

plane back home at Belgium's daybreak. "I'll be home for supper tomorrow night," he texted to her and began to pack, missing Caroline too much to sleep.

Caroline had filled every waking hour with Weddings Divine, decorating, and charity work. Those early morning phone calls sustained her through the day, but they didn't do much for her nights when dreams of Brandon would steal in and leave her wanting.

She missed him. Their relationship was less than ideal, but she was willing to have him on his terms. She could understand why trust would be an issue with him, and she was willing to be steadfast until he learned he could trust her. She had to move slowly, steadily, and consistently, showing him she would always be there for him, until he could learn to trust.

Brandon was worth it.

Weddings Divine had more business than she could handle. Ursula helped her find Heath and Heather. Heath had worked for one of the biggest party planners in the city, arranging krewe parties and debutante balls. Heather had been a high school youth counselor. The twin team wanted more autonomy, and Caroline gave it to them.

Heather handled brides and their mothers much better than Caroline ever did, and Heath's arrangements were truly divine.

Ursula proved more than competent. Her organizational skills were outstanding, and she accompanied Caroline to most of the charity functions so Caroline wasn't the odd duck out. Their friendship was growing each day, and Caroline realized how much different adult friendships were than those that grew from childhood familiarity.

At night, when she couldn't sleep, she would crochet blankets and booties, putting care into each stitch, hoping somehow the babies could feel her love for them.

Being an official Baby Cuddler gave more meaning to her life than she'd ever had. She had even given over some of Weddings Divine's inquiries to Heath and Heather when she could have gone herself rather than miss her shift at the hospital. She received as much benefit from the contact as the babies did.

She wouldn't have even thought about taking a pregnancy test if one of the neonatal nurses hadn't suggested it. Her symptoms of breast tenderness, roller-coaster emotions, and missed periods could all be explained away. The early morning nausea was a little harder to ignore.

She hadn't known that birth control was rendered ineffective when taking certain antibiotics like the one she had taken for her sniffles.

When the home pregnancy test came out positive, her world changed.

Chapter Fourteen

What was she going to do now?

Caroline let her tears mingle with the hot water that sprayed from all directions. She had no one to blame but herself.

Brandon's stance on babies, especially unplanned babies, was blatantly clear. And so was his belief in honoring agreements like their prenuptial agreement.

She had read through it so often in the last few hours that she'd memorized it.

The wife agrees to undergo and/or allow child to undergo testing to verify paternity of child. Should the husband be father of said child, wife agrees to relinquish custody in parentis and in loco. The wife further agrees that no child support or alimony will be due upon the dissolution of the marriage.

It had been written by one of the best lawyers in Louisiana. Jack's reputation was beyond dispute.

She didn't want Brandon's money. She only wanted her baby. But with Brandon's history, would he believe her? With his deep emotional scarring, *could* he believe her?

Brandon had never made any promises. He had never set

up false expectations or even tried to woo her with that lethal charisma of his. He'd simply been a companionable and generous housemate on top of fulfilling every term of their contract.

How had she forgotten, even for a second, that theirs was a relationship formed from words in a document, not emotions shared between soul mates. That's how she had started to think of him, as the man she was made to spend her life with. Obviously, she was the only one who felt that special bond she thought they had.

No one to blame but herself.

No matter how hard she tried, rubbing soap over her body couldn't erase the feel of his warm body next to hers. Her thighs still tingled where his hands had skimmed over them. Her breasts ached where his mouth had adored them. Her heart throbbed where he had captured it and made it his own.

She showered until her skin shriveled. What was she going to do now? What were the odds that their budding relationship could mature fast enough and deep enough to include parenthood, much less a forever marriage?

She could tell Brandon and hope he would throw out the pregnancy clause in their contract. Hope he wouldn't take her baby from her. In her heart, she thought he wouldn't. She believed he wasn't that kind of man. Right?

Everything she knew about Brandon indicated that the pregnancy clause came from Brandon trying to protect his offspring, not punish their mother. But she'd also seen him in action. Ruthless. He'd earned that reputation.

What did he really feel for her? Was that connection she felt between them really deep and abiding love? Love he wasn't ready to acknowledge yet? Or was it just her side of the heartbeat that felt that way? Was she superimposing her own desire to be loved into her guess about how Brandon felt about her?

Could she risk losing her baby on knowing Brandon less than a month?

Brandon considered his options. He could give up his first class seat and fly economy, sandwiched in like a sardine, and arrive three hours early. Or keep his roomy, first class seat and wait for his designated plane.

"Change the ticket," he growled.

Surely, three hours sitting and waiting at the airport would be worse than being in tight quarters for the sixteen-hour trip.

As he settled into his seat, squeezed between a well-fed grandmother and a well-known ex-wrestler, he wasn't so sure.

If nothing else proves my love to Caroline, this should. He dodged an elbow as Grandma opened her newspaper, only to end up practically in the lap of the wrestler.

"Sorry." He straightened up, pulling in his shoulders as tight as he could.

"No problem." The wrestler patted him on the knee. "I didn't notice a ring. Involved with anyone?"

Sixteen hours of misery. The only way he would make it through this hellish flight was remembering that his own personal angel awaited him on the other side.

"Crème brulee? What's the occasion?" Ursula spooned up a bite and moaned in pleasure. "This is better than an orgasm."

Caroline grinned. "Then you need a better lover."

"He's that good?"

"Yes, he is. At least as far as I know, he is. Since Brandon was my first, I really don't have much to compare it to." Caroline drew lines in her own crème brulee with her spoon. "I've got a problem."

"Let's hear it, friend."

"I'm pregnant."

Ursula stirred her own brulee. "And why is that a problem?"

Caroline handed over her copy of her prenup. "Brandon married me to lose his bachelor status and get the media off his back."

"And you married Brandon because…?"

"Because I was broke and he promised to pay off all my debts."

"I still don't see the problem."

"Our marriage is only supposed to last six months. Then we have an amicable divorce and go our own ways. Except, now, this comes into play." Caroline pointed to the conception clause of the prenup. "Brandon gets to keep my baby."

"That's not what is says. Where's the six month clause?"

"It's a handshake agreement. The terms are implied in the prenuptial contract. See that part about how much alimony I get after six months? And the part about any terms of this contract shall not be not be contested by either party should this arrangement end in divorce?"

Caroline crossed her arms over her bloated stomach. Even though her baby was only microscopic, her doctor had told her that swollen stomachs and lost waistlines came early for some women. Since she was so small, she would show earlier than most.

Then there was the nausea. The fleeting thought she'd had this morning about hiding her pregnancy for a while flushed away along with her morning sickness. She might be able to cover either her shape changes or her new morning toilet hugging ritual, but not both. Brandon was too acute for that.

She twisted her napkin. "What if I get a divorce before he finds out I'm pregnant?"

"Is that what you want? To leave Brandon?"

"No. But I'm not giving up my baby."

Ursula scanned the papers again, to the front sheet and then back to the Conception Clause. "You need a lawyer to interpret this."

"Know any good ones."

"As a matter of fact…."

"I'm pretty sure Jack would see a conflict of interest should I try to hire him."

"I wasn't talking about Jack." Ursula shuffled through a few cards in her card case, then pulled out a dog-eared, yellowed one that read Arthur Alexander Sanders, Attorney at Law. "Call Alex."

"I won't have the money to pay him. Even though Weddings Divine is doing well, I'll owe Brandon for all the money he advanced me. We haven't had a chance to entrench ourselves in the market yet. And who's to say we'll keep getting clients when I'm no longer Mrs. Brandon D'Estrehan."

"Not to worry. He'll do it pro bono."

"You sound so certain."

"He's my half-brother."

"Jack will be pleased to know that."

Ursula grinned like the cat who ate the canary. "Jack will have to figure out that one on his own." She folded up the contract and handed it back to Caroline. "So what's your plan?"

"Plan? I haven't had time to think. He'll be home tonight, and I need to get away. Have some time to sort things out."

Ursula clasped Caroline's hand. "Are you sure this will be a problem? I'm getting very strong vibes that Brandon's really into you."

"I thought so, too. But I've only known him for a little over a month. I can't risk my baby."

"Why are you so sure it's a risk?"

"Before he left, I told him I loved him. He didn't appear happy to hear it."

Ursula leaned forward, earnestness in her voice. "He has a right to know about his child."

Caroline twisted her wedding ring on her finger. "I'll let him know about the baby, of course, but not right away. I need some time to get used to the idea myself. I need to talk to your brother to verify if an immediate divorce will get me around this clause. Then I need to figure out how I'm going to raise this child alone. When I have a plan, I'll let him know. Right now, I'm not sure what I'll do. All I know for certain is that my baby will have so much love he or she will never doubt for one second that it was wanted."

"In addition to calling my brother, what do you need me to do to help?"

"Brandon's flight will land tonight at eight o'clock. I need to be sure of what I'm going to do, or he'll make plans so fast I won't be able to stop him." Caroline glanced at their wedding photo sitting on the sideboard. "Like the wedding."

"He did pull that off quickly." Ursula nodded. "You can stay with me, of course.

"I need to be somewhere he can't find me until I'm ready to be found. But I don't have anywhere to go. You've traveled all over. I was hoping you could help. Otherwise, I'm going to put my finger on a map and there I'll be."

"If you're determined to go, I'd rather know you were safe. I've got a friend who has a tea shop in an artsy part of Taos, New Mexico. She rents rooms above her shop."

Caroline grabbed Ursula's hands. "Thank you. And please, promise me you won't tell him."

"Brandon would never hurt you."

"Of course he wouldn't. But he could try to coerce me into something I don't want to do."

"I'll promise not to tell if you'll promise to contact him when you've got your plans figured out."

"Deal."

Brandon arrived in New Orleans at five o'clock. He'd never flown coach internationally before, and he never wanted to do it again.

But cashing in his first class ticket for the cramped space, the sleepless night, and the plastic food would be worth it to see Caroline three hours earlier than planned. He wanted a kiss, supper, and a hot shower in that order.

He missed her so much that he was imagining her. If he hadn't known better, as he rushed by a gate loading passengers to New Mexico, he could have sworn the petite brunette was her.

Giving her this two-and-a-half weeks of space had almost killed him. But that's all the distance he could stand from her, emotionally as well as physically. He loved her.

He didn't know when it had happened or how. He was only certain that it had. Two dozen times a day, he had wanted to pick up the phone to tell her. But declaring undying love wasn't something a man did over the phone.

He wasn't at all certain he could be the kind of husband, the kind of man, Caroline deserved. But he was very certain that he would try, every second of every day of his life, to be worthy of her love.

He would rip up their prenuptial contract and tell her that everything he had, his body, mind and soul, and all his worldly possessions were hers to have and to hold.

Too tired to drive, he climbed into the back of a cab and closed his eyes. When the driver jerked to a stop, he blearily came to his senses, handed over some big bills without bothering to count, and felt his weariness lift knowing he was home and Caroline was on the other side of his door.

The house was dark and quiet.

"Caroline?" His voice faded into the shadows.

"Caroline?" This time he shouted loud enough to raise the ghosts.

A heavy blanket of worry began to grow around his heart. He checked the dining room table. Nothing.

But their wedding photo was gone.

After finding her wedding ring on his nightstand, he was certain she had left him. The note attached to the divorce documents on his desk said it all.

> *I'm sorry. This isn't working for me. I'll pay the money back somehow.*
>
> *C.*

Brandon roared in pain and rage. She hadn't even bothered to sign her name.

That was it. One hundred and eighty uncontested days and their marriage would be over.

His pride said "Let her go." His preservation instinct asked "How will you live without your heart?" The cold, empty place in his chest was all the proof he needed that Caroline had taken it with her.

What was he going to do now?

A disorienting wave of indecision swept over him.

Jet lag. It had to be jet lag. He could always think on his feet. Turning around, he headed for his front door.

Ursula would know where she was. She was Caroline's PA. She should know everything.

Twinkle lights guided him up the stairs to the front door of the quadplex, mocking him in their nonsensical cheerfulness.

He knocked on the door hard enough to make the two plants on either side quiver in their urns.

A tall, thin fellow with dreadlocks and a happy grin answered. "Can I help you?"

"Where's Ursula?"

At Brandon's tone, the man lost his smile. His scowl would have intimidated a lesser man. "Who wants to know?"

"Her boss."

"Caroline D'Estrehan is her boss. You don't look like Caroline to me."

As much as Brandon wanted to take his frustration out on this human roadblock, he didn't have the time to strong-arm this guy. "My wife is missing. Where is Ursula?"

"That's different." The man's face changed from challenge to worry. "She's next door. If you need any help…"

"Thanks." Brandon took off as fast as his new spurt of adrenaline could carry him.

Jack met him at the front door, mint julep in hand, Ursula standing behind him looking thoroughly kissed. "You're home a bit early."

"Caroline's gone." Had Brandon ever uttered bleaker words? Saying it aloud made it too real, too painful. He grasped the doorframe to keep himself on his feet.

"I know." Jack stood aside. "Come in. We were relaxing on the back deck."

Brandon entered, taking the drink Jack pressed on him without thought, and followed his host through the house to the intimate setting of cushioned chairs, wicker tables, and fans swirling lazily to keep away the insects and humidity.

Brandon dropped into a chair, and Ursula took the one opposite him. For the first time in his life, Brandon let his emotions show on his face. Anguish etched lines and grooves, and he didn't even try to smooth them away.

"Why?" Absently, he sipped from his glass. "What did I do?"

Ursula took his hand. In his pain, he jerked from her

touch, but then tightened his fingers around hers. Compassion shined from her eyes. "Are you sure it wasn't something you didn't do? Something you didn't say?"

Brandon sat on the edge of his seat. "What do you mean?"

"Does she know what she means to you?"

"I was getting to that part." He looked down into his glass, twirling it in his hand.

"A woman doesn't like to wait on the words, especially if she can't be sure."

"I didn't want to move too fast."

"Ha! Who was it that proposed and married in the same day? You move fast enough when it suits you."

Brandon had the grace to look sheepish. "I'll fix it. I'll make it right. Just tell me where she is."

"A woman appreciates a man who puts out effort for her. You've got the world at your fingertips. Maybe it's time you had to work for a woman." Ursula squeezed his hand. "I sound harsh, I know. I'm sorry. But Caroline needs time to think, and I promised her I wouldn't tell."

"She's safe?"

"Yes, of course."

"If you talk to her—"

"You'll tell her yourself when you find her."

He tried to formulate a plan in his mind, but the long hours, the stress, the grief all came crashing down on him. The thought of going home to his empty house and crawling into his bed seemed impossible. The memory of Caroline on their wedding night was branded into his pillowcases and sheets.

Ursula put on soothing music, and she and Jack quietly played rummy while keeping him company, but all he did was sit and stare out into the night.

After carrying so much on his shoulders for so long, everything in his life was crashing down around him because

Caroline wasn't there. A great depression sat on his chest and weighed down his eyelids, leaving him with nothing but empty blackness.

He awoke on Jack's back porch with a headache that made him squint against the early morning sun. The noises of the neighborhood had him gritting his teeth in pain. A night spent sleeping in the deck chair made him stiff and sore.

And heartache made his world as dark and grey and out of control as a hurricane.

Over the next few days, Brandon focused all his attention on finding Caroline. If not for Jack, mergers would have fallen through, profits would have tumbled instead of climbed, and employees would have had their heads snapped off at the slightest infraction.

Brandon used every means of search at his considerable disposal. How could she just disappear?

Airline security made tracing her through flights impossible. Taking a bus or a car could be done without leaving an identity trail. Surveillance and discreet inquiry to her parents served no purpose. He tried to trace Caroline through her credit cards, but she hadn't used them. What was she using for money? What was she doing to survive?

He was exhausted. Trying to sleep in his penthouse brought about the same problems as trying to sleep in his bed. Memories of Caroline and regrets of how he had walked out on her after she declared her love made him toss and turn until finally he had to run to escape his own thoughts.

Most nights he ended up on Jack's deck. Ursula had taken pity on him and convinced Jack to buy a comfortable pool lounger for the deck, so at least he could stretch out a bit.

For the fourth night in a row, Ursula served a recipe that she claimed was native to New Mexico. If Brandon hadn't been raised on the spicy food of Louisiana, his stomach would be in shreds by now.

"I hear the artwork coming out of Taos is spectacular. You should make a trip to see it."

Sarcastically, he told her. "Sightseeing isn't on my schedule. Why don't you tell me where Caroline is?"

"Because I promised not to." She gave him another helping of blue corn chips to go with his green chile salsa. "You might find a real treasure. And there's this little hangout that I got this salsa recipe from. Definitely worth the trip."

Finally, Brandon wrapped his mind around the clues Ursula had been dropping for the last few days.

"That's where she is, isn't it?"

"I promised not to tell, remember? But if you find you're in Taos, be sure to visit my friend's tea house. The crumpets are exquisite."

After too many sleepless nights and a quick flight—economy class again—he now sat in a teahouse in Taos, New Mexico, watching Caroline wait tables. It was a ladies' tea room. The chairs were too delicate, the servers' aprons too frilly, and he was too keyed up to relax. The work seemed to suit her, though. As usual she was calm, taking the busy crowd in stride, but she had a glow about her. Was she really content? Hadn't she missed him at all?

Caroline could feel the weight of a stare as she balanced three plates and a pitcher of water. She turned and had to do a quick step to keep from dropping the lot on the floor.

Brandon!

He'd found her. Her heart pumped with elation while her stomach twisted with dread. What did this mean?

Falling back on his trick of business as usual, she walked over to his table and said, "What can I get you?"

Her voice came out a little ragged around the edges, and her order pad shook in her hand, but she thought she was doing rather well. Her knees were holding her up, and her stiff neck was keeping her chin high.

"We need to talk."

"I'm working."

"Take a break."

"The boss is watching."

"I'll buy the damned restaurant."

"Is that how you think it's done? You can get anything you want for a price?" She swallowed and admitted, "You've good reason to think that with me, I guess. But I'm no longer for sale."

"It's not like that between us."

"It's exactly like that between us. You'll either have to order or leave."

Brandon pointedly looked at all the other patrons nursing a single cup of tea while they typed away on their laptops or chatted with friends. "This is ridiculous, Caroline. You don't need to be doing this."

"Yes, I do. For my pride." She spoke to another customer who had just taken a seat. "I'll be right with you." Then she turned back to Brandon. "Order?"

"Bring me coffee."

"We only serve tea."

"Fine. Tea."

"What kind?"

"It doesn't matter." He tapped his fingers on the table.

"Coming right up."

Caroline also took the order of the newcomer, stalling to give herself time to think, then slowly headed back to the kitchen.

The cook, a college weight lifter, asked, "Is he hassling you? Do I need to get rid of him?"

She didn't think, even with all his bulk, he was capable of getting rid of Brandon if her husband wanted to stay.

"No. I can handle him." And she could, she realized. She was in charge of her own destiny.

Through the shutters separating the kitchen from the dining area, Caroline watched Brandon twirl his wedding ring around on his finger.

Brandon had never fiddled before. She had always marveled at how still he sat, never giving any sign of emotion. Dark circles ringed his eyes, and lines bracketed his mouth. How long had it been since he last slept?

She delivered her orders, setting down his tea last.

He took a sip. "Decaf?"

"Yes."

The horrible tea gave him hope. "What time do you get off?"

"I'm working a double. I've got a debt to repay."

"No, Caroline. No debt."

"If that's all," she smoothed down her apron, "I have to check on my other customers."

"Sugar."

"Pardon me?"

"I need sugar for my tea."

"You drink your tea plain."

"Maybe I've changed." He looked up at her, his hands wrapped around his cup as if to keep them in place. "You've changed me, Caroline. I want you to come back home."

She wanted him, too. She wanted to reach out and smooth away the lines in his forehead. To sit down and listen to all his concerns. To try to ease his burdens.

To share this baby with him.

Was being wanted enough? Could she settle for want? Would it fade or turn into resentment when he found out about the baby? That's what entrapment had done to his parents. She whirled away. "I'll be back with your sugar."

Instead, she fled to the employees' lounge. Tears trickled down her face as she realized that she couldn't settle, not for herself, but especially not for her baby. Brandon was used to getting what he wanted, so hearing no wouldn't sit well with him, but that's what he'd have to accept.

She would tell him about the baby, of course, after that damned divorce was final and his hold on her was null and void. After her heart was strong enough to just be friends for the sake of their child.

Splashing water on her face erased the tracks of her tears, but plain water couldn't erase the misery in her eyes.

The door flung open as she reapplied mascara, and she jumped. Without looking up, she said, "I'll be done in just a second."

"I'll wait." Brandon's deep voice filled the room. "I'll wait forever, if that's what I need to do."

She turned to him, hope blossoming. "Why?"

He caught her hand in his and looked down into her eyes. "Because I love you."

He handed her a large box. When she opened it she found a huge magnolia blossom inside. On the stem was her discarded wedding ring.

She untied her apron, letting him see the slight bulge under her shirt. When his eyes grew wide and darkened, she knew he understood. "Are you sure?"

With awe, he put a hand over her stomach. His face stretched into the happiest smile she'd ever seen. "Yes. I love you both."

"You don't feel trapped? I can care for this baby on my own."

"I feel like I've received the best gift a man could ever get. I swear to you, I will try to be worthy every day of my life. It will be my privilege to care for my child." He knelt down on one knee. "Will you marry me again?"

"Yes. I will marry you again."

He patted her stomach, "I hate to ask, but could we have a rushed wedding?"

"Of course. Rushed weddings are my specialty."

Also by Connie Cox

Single Titles

Taking Flight
Contractually Yours
White Wine and Wild Rides (coming soon)

Medical Romances

The Baby Who Saved Dr. Cynical
Return of the Rebel Surgeon
His Hidden American Beauty
When the Cameras Stop Rolling...
Christmas Eve Delivery

White Wine & Wild Roses

Coming soon...

Wanna be a rock star...

When rollercoaster junkie Selena Ramirez agrees to help her rockstar boss by becoming her body double, she doesn't bank on loving her new glamorous look. Nor does she bank on the attraction she feels for Blair's friend and boutique winery owner Eric Saunders.

Enthralled by the dynamic Blair since the beginning of her career, Eric has allowed the world to believe he's Blair's boyfriend in order to protect the rising rock star. Concerned by his friend's exhaustion, he begrudgingly agrees to perpetuate the lie by pretending Selena is Blair during a weeklong getaway, but when the contrived kisses and romantic dinners start feeling all too real, Eric realizes he wants something real with Selena.

Addicted to wild rides, Selena prides herself on keeping the safety bar in place and her hands in the air, but buckling in with her boss's man makes the tracks ahead feel dangerous. And if she's not careful, she just might take the plunge...toward love.

Sign up for my newsletter and be the first to learn about newest releases, contests, and giveaway.

www.conniecox.com

www.ingramcontent.com/pod-product-compliance
Lightning Source LLC
Chambersburg PA
CBHW071717140626
46557CB00012B/940